EITHE'S WAY

RHIAN WALLER

First published by The Write Factor, 2014
www.thewritefactor.co.uk

A CIP catalogue record for this book is available from
the British Library.

Cover and design by Six:Eight Design
www.sixeight.co.uk

I want to dedicate this book — with all its absent parents — to my father, who would have been there if he could have been, and my mother, who is always there.

About the Author

Rhian Waller has been using words to jump into other worlds since she learned to read. In time, she decided that she would like to create some worlds of her own so other people could visit them. She is 29 and lives in North Wales, where she teaches, writes for a local newspaper and plays with poetry and short stories. She has placed more than 40 of these in e-zines, print zines and magazines. This is her first novel.

Foreword

RHIAN WALLER'S FIRST NOVEL, Eithe's Way won
The Write Factor's annual Shortlist Award, 2014. The
panel of judges were impressed by Waller's sublime turns
of phrase: "… his smile thickened and lengthened like a
feeding leech", and also her ability to build a palpable sense
of tension and foreboding in the narrative. Waller has a
precocious talent that belies her years; she writes with
great wisdom and has a way with words that makes one
hopeful that this is the first of many great novels.

The Write Factor was founded to support the writing
process. To encourage previously unpublished writers and
give them a foothold on the publishing ladder, The Write
Factor holds a Shortlist competition on a given subject,
every year.

The Award is presented to the writer judged to have the most flair and talent. Their short story or book is then published and promoted by The Write Factor, giving the winner a platform from which to launch their writing career.

For more details visit www.thewritefactor.co.uk

Lorna Howarth
Founding Editor, The Write Factor

Contents

EITHE'S WAY

Twenty Years Ago

Beginning at the Beginning

MRS DORD WAS IN PAIN. The pain was so huge that it filled all of her, but she didn't want to scream, because if she did that, then her husband would call an ambulance, and then she would have to go to hospital. She did not want to go to hospital. She didn't believe in hospitals. She believed in the intelligence of her own body, in the value of herbal cures and home birthing. She did not want starched sheets and metal things inside her.

Mr Dord paced outside the door, and as the wave of pain ebbed, she said between gritted teeth: 'Dear, will you fetch me another cup of chamomile, meadowsweet and willow bark? And the golden seal.'

Then she bit down on her own blanket as another contraction began. Why, she wondered, between grunts and huffs, was it called golden seal? It was supposed to strengthen her contractions and speed up her un-sealing. And it wasn't all that golden, either.

Her husband hurried away. He was a quiet, gentle man with tight-curled hair and dark skin, and she'd brought him to a tiny village and, through the sheer strength of will, shamed the gossips because *it was rude to stare*.

She suppressed a grunt, but something was tearing inside her, and there was a gush of blood that had nothing to do with breaking waters. She began to scream, properly scream, not just moan and wail. Mr Dord burst into the room, slopping hot tea up his arm. He didn't seem to notice.

'Oh God,' he said, when he saw the mess. 'I'm going to phone an ambulance.'

'No,' she hiccuped, as she crested a wave of pain.

It was a testament to how highly he regarded her opinion that he hesitated for a second, but there was so much blood, and he'd never been so afraid in his life. He dialled on the bedroom telephone.

'No!' screamed Mrs Dord, and despite the pain, she dragged herself on to all fours and crawled across the bed toward him, one hand snatching. Her hot, damp fingers almost knocked the phone from his grasp, but something in her abdomen snagged. After that, she couldn't speak.

In the ambulance, she recited both versions of the baby-name under her breath, one for a boy, one for a girl. They were quite short, so she had to stretch them to fit them into a mantra. Ten minutes later she was in a white room on top of a white sheet that rapidly turned red. Mrs Dord, her mouth stuffed with tubes and covered with an oxygen mask, slipped in and out of consciousness.

When she half-woke, he was looking down at her and crying unashamedly.

'You have to choose the name,' he said. 'Just in case. I can't decide. You have to do it.'

She couldn't speak through the oxygen mask, but she nodded, ever so slightly. The doctors had put something in her to bring the pain down, and it was making her feel strange. *Silly, lovely man*, she thought. *Just in case what? I'm not going to die.*

Mr Dord turned to the nurse. 'Have you got a piece of paper?' he said, 'and a pencil?' The nurse fetched him a pad and pen, passing them over with a mixture of pity and efficiency. Mr Dord pushed them under his wife's hand, the one that wasn't pierced by the drip needle. She began to write in large, wavering letters. The child was going to be called Jane or John, she'd decided, right from the start. Something simple and strong.

She began to write 'either', because she'd refused a scan to find out the sex of the baby, but before she completed the first word, her eyes rolled up into her skull. The last thing she heard before she passed out was her husband's perplexed voice.

'Ee-thee?' he said, and she thought, *no*, then she died.

EITHE'S WAY

Not So Long Ago

The List

DETECTIVE INSPECTOR KEANE WAS NOT happy. She stood by her desk, her knuckles pressing the plastic as though she was imprinting her territory. 'Don't see why I have to be co-opted. Not my specialty. Don't know a thing about finance. Can't some toss-bucket from upstairs do it?' she said, gruffly.

'No,' said the Superintendent. 'It's orders from higher-up. You're being re-assigned. I know it's not a great time for you, but everyone's feeling the pinch. We all have to muck-in.'

'This isn't the way of things,' said Keane. 'Too fast. Something's not right.'

'Think of it as a sideways promotion,' the Superintendent made a one-shoulder shrug. 'Oh, and here.' He passed her an envelope. 'A golden handshake, I'd imagine.'

Keane waited until he left before she tore open the gummed flap. There was a piece of paper inside. She pulled it out and unfolded it. It read:

Joshua, Dale High, year 11. Football, rugby. Walks to school.
Daniel, Everpool Controlled Primary, year 4. Choir, chess. School bus catchment area. Departs 8.15 pm from Stanley Street.

The list continued for another thirty lines. Keane's usually florid face flushed a deeper shade of red. There was no name at the bottom of the letter, only a single sentence:

We will be in touch.

Stranger in
the Station

THE SECOND-HAND DRESS HUNG FROM the top
of the door. It was off-white and smelled musty. Eithe
touched it with one finger. The pressure of old silk
screamed against her skin. Her head throbbed and her
tongue felt toxic. The bed covers were awry. Without
trying, she could close her eyes and imagine Joe-of-
half-an-hour-ago slip from the mattress, move into the
bathroom and open the cabinet. She could hear him clean
his teeth, with little retching sounds as the brush hit his
soft palate, and then the gurgle and spit of mouthwash.

Where was he?

She brought the hanger down, her hand trembling, and posed in front of the full-length mirror, the dress brought up to her chin. She stood in stasis until a shudder riddled her bones. The dress hit the carpet. She wrenched open the drawers, scrabbled through the wardrobe for the carry case and blindly shoved handfuls of underwear into it. She stopped to look up and listen for an instant.

A key slid into the lock. She heard the bitings grind against the pins. Each click of metal was a hammer on an anvil. Her head turned toward the sound and fear sliced through the nausea, bright and shining and as sharp as a needle.

The sash window above the dresser was open. She grabbed the case, stopping to snatch up her driver's license and passport, clambered up on to the polished wood, put her leg over the window sill and squeezed through. She was tall, so it was a tight fit, and she fell onto the fire escape in a tangle of gangling limbs. She picked herself up and did a stupid down-the-stairs tiptoeing run to the ground. Her feet skittered on the slimy concrete of the back alley, and she pushed her way out of the forest of recycling bins and fled.

Hours later, her half-empty drag-along case bounced and clattered as it hit the lines between the tiles. Paddington Station was choked. Some people smelled of body odour and bad breath laced with hunger. She followed the surge as it swept her past turnstiles and timetables, and down a long corridor where she collided with a man. It was like slamming into a tree-trunk.

'Ouch,' she said.

'Excuse me,' said the body. His voice was turned-off and utterly distracted. The rest of the crowd broke around them like surf as, for a moment, curiosity overrode her panic. She followed his gaze. It bored through the glass which protected a dead LCD billboard. His reflection was clear on the blank surface. Little prickles of unease slid through her skin.

Her first thought was that he was homeless, except that his suit, ruckled at the ankles and wrists, was designer. She waved an experimental hand past his gaze.

'Excuse me,' he said. It was a reflex, something said a dozen times an hour to the pedestrians bouncing off his bulk.

'Sir, why are you just standing there? Don't you need to get somewhere?' The seconds ticked by. 'What are you looking at?'

His smile spread, thickened and lengthened like a feeding leech. Eithe saw what was wrong. Her stomach tightened and she felt something cold swim down her spine, because the man staring out of the glass screen was not smiling.

She asked, 'Is it a trick?'

'No,' said the man staring into the mirror.

'How is it happening?'

She heard strain in her voice because her refuge was the rational, and there was nothing rational about a reflection which would not obey physics. Maybe there was something wrong with the screen. Perhaps it was glitching. Her fingertips met in the glass, and his reflection turned to look at her. His stare was molten and black.

'Why?'

'Part of me,' said the man. The muscles of his jaw bunched and slackened. 'It's gone.'

She jogged his arm. 'How are you doing this?'

He did not look away from the screen. She reached up and took his head in her hands. They were almost of a

height, and he was weak and wilting from days without
sleep or food. It felt strange to be so close to a man who
was not Joe. His cheeks were bristled and his skin felt
damp and unhealthy, as though he had a cold fever. Gently,
she eased his face from the window, cupping her fingers
to funnel his gaze. He resisted at first, but then he broke
contact and his pupils latched on to hers.

'There,' she said. Around them, the crowd parted and
fused back together. She took her hands away.

'I'm Eithe,' she said.

'I don't know my name. I think I lost it. I leaned too far
in and I dropped it.'

The staring man frowned until a thick line pushed
into the skin between his brows, deep, like a knife wound.
Impossibly, in the curve of his cornea and the dark of his
iris, she saw nothing, not her own face, no glint of light,
nothing, except a gaping vacuum.

'I'm going to have to go now,' she said, suddenly afraid
again. 'I'm sorry. I don't know how to help you.' As she
turned and walked away, she didn't notice the reflection
leave the glass, or that the man stared into blankness.

She was about ten yards into the forecourt when there
was a sound of heavy cloth hitting the floor. She looked
over her shoulder. The man lay in a heap. Eithe took a
step back, then away, and then she hovered, inadequate,
uncertain, paralysed by her lack of competence. She didn't
know if she should put something under his head and take
his pulse or if she would just get in the way. An attendant
in a high visibility jacket arrived and knelt by the sprawled
casualty. A clump of people gathered. Eithe sloped off.

The alien reflection followed her down the corridor,
distorting in the plastic cases of the rolling billboard
advertisements, dappled by the plastic of a water bottle

held by a toddler, stretched into thin strips by the metal handrail. She grasped her case and hurried on. His feet followed the bottom of hers, step for step, but she didn't notice. In the main terminal, she paused and stared up at the Departures board. She looked for a very long time.

The first notes of *Ten Green Bottles* played, and she went into her bag, shuffling through underwear and hastily packed toiletries until her hand closed around her phone. The tip of her forefinger wavered over the button. She bit her lip. The little tune played out and started again. She stood there, tiny beneath a night held high by the steel struts of the arching roof, one undecided speck in a spill and spin of people who knew exactly where they wanted to go.

Eventually, he gave up, but a little chirrup prompted her to check her texts.

Come back to me.

She put the phone away and sat on the floor with her back to the wall, her coat pulled up to her chin, her arms hard around the case on her lap, and fell into a fitful sleep. Strange eyes watched her through windows, belt buckles, coins and a thin sheen of spilled water guarded by a yellow easel and its WARNING letters.

Her dreams were vivid.

Once, she woke and a face that wasn't hers looked back at her from the curved Perspex of a newspaper stand and said, 'I lost the way. Do you know where it is?', but she knew it couldn't be real and she fell back into her turbulent visions. With Joe's threats still crackling in her brain, she dreamed about death – about how the bowels and bladder relaxed and evacuated, about the smells, the gurgling and the rigor mortis.

Nobody noticed her, until a hand landed on her shoulder. She jolted awake.

'Are you all right?' The policeman looked closely at Eithe, who fidgeted.

She thought about all of the other things the man must see on his beat, drunken fights with teeth rolling across the pavement, women with torn clothes and faces, kids puking on the street, neighbours burning each other's sheds down over fencing disputes, puddles of blood and piss and cold, stiff, sad people lying blue and silent in the gutter. Somehow, all of it seemed bigger and harder than her ill-defined fear and the twisting in her guts.

'I'll be all right,' she said.

'You can't sleep here,' he said, and he left.

Her teeth were furry. She paid a pound to use a toilet cubicle, brought out a toothbrush and started to tidy herself up under the sick violet light. She was building a fine white lather when she looked up at the mirror. It should have been her own self, a face framed by curling hair, her skin an indifferent taupe, her wide lips slightly chapped from her nervous habit of sucking on them. But that wasn't who she saw.

She recognised him at once.

Her teeth clenched hard on the brush and her face shut down with shock. A little foam leaked from her mouth.

'Don't scream,' he said.

The Mess Left Behind

THE FLAT WAS A MORASS of ash and empty wrappers because Joe was too miserable and too superstitious to clean up. He had been vegetarian for years. Now burger boxes littered every surface, and greasy kebab papers lay on the floor. He hated them as relics of his failure, but perhaps if the mess stayed, she would have to come back and clean for him.

He drank because it made the anger burn. Anger was simple.

He smoked because the government wouldn't let him do it in the pub any more, and he hated politicians, with their hypocrisy and their back-room business buddies and their publically funded duck-houses and moats.

He watched the blue coils twist toward the
stained ceiling.

He and Eithe shared the flat for years, ever since they
graduated. He hadn't been able to find a job, or pay off
his university debt, and they wouldn't have been offered a
mortgage. He was going to become a social worker, and
he applied for posts up and down the country, but with so
little experience and so many veteran workers redundant,
he'd failed time after time. He remained a Jobseeker,
attended his climate change awareness meetings, and the
Young Socialists and his direct action group, where they
had to pull the batteries out of their phones in case the
authorities accessed them remotely and listened in. So he
and Eithe stayed in the same grotty flat and dreamed of a
better future.

But the strange, solemn little girl from the other side
of the fence was gone. His wife-to-be was gone and she'd
taken his future with her.

She had no money and only the clothes she ran away
with, second hand threads that he'd picked for her from
Scope and Oxfam while she was at work. He thought
about what lay beneath her clothes. He thought about a
stranger touching her. The stranger might have used his
fingers. Joe would break them, one by one. The stranger
might have kissed her. Joe would take his cigarette lighter
and burn those lips to weeping scabs. The stranger might
have fucked her.

Joe's breath streaked grey from between his teeth.

He got up and stalked around the room. His limbs
quivered with nicotine and hate and, to his horror, a trickle
of arousal.

Eithe was quiet, she did not impose. She had no mass,
she presented no resistance to the wind. She was fragile,

and the sun shone through her. She made no marks. She was the sort to die quietly.

He lit another cigarette. The ember flared orange as he breathed in. He drew the duvet around him like a meaty cocoon.

His nightmares were ghastly. Joe was sitting at his mother's kitchen table with a copy of the *Communist Manifesto*. Everything in the room was big; the tablecloth was a blue field, the flaws on the cupboard doors distorted into toothy mouths and the shining knobs on the door and drawers winked with eyes. He was wary and kept the cover out of view, but he had to carry on reading, with that strange dream-compulsion which makes people leap out of towers or count worthless coins over and over and over.

He read the sentences but couldn't remember them, because dream books don't hold written words – though he knew it was the *Communist Manifesto* because of the dream prescience that convinced him that Mr King would come bursting through the door.

His belly lurched as the behemoth crashed into the room, filling it from corner to corner with broken veins, bristling nasal hairs and barely-dammed anger.

A massive hand scooped down and pulled up the book. Joe reached for it with feeble fingers, but he was too weak. Mr King thrust him aside with one hand, the other clutched around the neck of a black bin bag. Inside, more of Joe's books struggled, the corners piercing the plastic, their spines arching against their prison, and they screamed. It was the sound of tearing paper and grief.

Joe ran after him, but the floor turned into ash so fine his feet sank into it, and he couldn't follow.

4

A Bargain

'AND DON'T RUN,' SAID THE man from the mirror.

She took a step back. The toothbrush dropped out of her jaw and landed in the bowl. She retired to the nearest toilet, and sat there, head in hands.

'What's your name?' he said.

'Hahaha.' Her laugh was horrifyingly flat.

'Tell me.'

'Eithe,' she said.

'Evie,' he said, in a voice like a wet finger sliding on glass.

'Eithe.'

'Aofie,' he tried again.

'It's Ee-thee. Go away!' she shouted, loud enough
for the people in the next cubicles to hear. Maybe the
absurdity of it unwound her nerves, or perhaps she'd
used up her reserve of emotion, but she quieted down.
The fingers in her hair quaked. 'You're the Mirror Man,'
she said.

'You ran into me,' he said, 'the flesh part of me.'

'Then what are you?'

'The mind part, I think.'

Her nostrils flared.

'You haven't gone mad,' he said.

Then she surprised herself by laughing. 'The voice in
my head is telling me I'm sane.'

'You are,' said the Mirror Man, desperately.

'Perhaps I'm mad, although I can't be mad because
mad people don't think they're mad, so I'm not,' she said.
She held on to the idea tight, curling around it, afraid
that it would trickle away like sand in a clenched hand.
'I can't deal with this right now,' she said. 'I was supposed
to get married next week. I had a dress, and a maid of
honour, and a hen-do with people from work who I didn't
really know, which I shouldn't have gone on, and I had a
husband-to-be. Now I don't know what to do. I haven't got
anyone to go to, or anywhere to go. I'm alone. I've never
been alone, and now I am.'

The Mirror Man said, 'Don't tell anyone you see me.
They will lock you up.'

'What are you?' she said, very quietly.

'I'm stuck.'

'And I'm stranded,' she said. 'My boyfriend stripped my
bank account.'

'Then we have something in common.'

'Of course we do,' she said. 'I invented you because I'm scared and lonely, and I don't have any friends.'

'No you didn't,' said the Mirror Man.

'Prove it,' said Eithe.

'You need a place to stay,' he said. He sounded more confident now they were negotiating.

'Yes,' said Eithe.

'Then you can stay in my flat. There's no one there at the moment. I promise you'll be safe.'

'This is stupid,' said Eithe.

'Sleeping in a train station on your own is stupid,' said the Mirror Man. Eithe thought about the hard floor and her vulnerability, about the grimy feeling beneath her unwashed clothes.

'Okay.'

The Mirror Man was with her on the Tube train, where the rails spat sparks. He looked as bored as every other commuter at the roll-call of stations, but to Eithe they were strange names, Tooting Bec, Goodge and Morden. She saw him in every bright surface as they exited from London Bridge station into the South Bank, and in the puddles, and in the windows on the way to his high rise.

Someone had sprayed the word 'TWAT' across the intercom, and someone else with a slightly more refined hand had added: 'Wit of a banker' below the penthouse buzzer.

'It's a spoonerism,' the Mirror Man sighed. 'Written by someone with too much time on their hands.'

He told her the combination for the door, and waited with her as the lift ascended.

The flat on the top floor was dark and dusty, but it was large for somewhere near the centre of the city. Eithe's feet sank into the carpet. Expensive prints hung on the walls

– photographs of Jeff Koons' soulless vacuum cleaners and a pastiche of Warhol's endless, pointless self-replication, except that it was the Mirror Man looking out of the canvas, blodged with primaries and neons. There were also framed photographs of him shaking hands with a lot of different men. She didn't recognise any of them, although they were wearing very nice suits and they all looked quite smug. There was a lot of chrome and a huge, shatterproof pane of glass looking out over the London skyline. In the middle distance, the Thames flowed. She could see the OXO tower, and behind that the Eye glaring back at her, white and blank as a cataract.

'I am real,' said the Mirror Man from the window. Little points of light shone through him. 'This is my home.'

Eithe looked around. It was not very homely. The prints were alienating and there were no ornaments. It looked like a page from a Habitat catalogue.

'Make yourself some food, if you can find any,' he said.

There were flax seed and nori crackers in the cupboard and a jar of organic pasta sauce. Eithe ate it out of its container, perched on a leather sofa in front of a television that was big enough to crush a grown human. The Mirror Man looked out of the screen. 'It's a Super Hi-Vision eight-k TV, developed by NHK. Top of the range. Cutting edge. What do you think?'

Eithe shrugged.

'For fuck's sake,' he said, affronted. 'Can't you see how much it cost?'

'But you can't watch it,' she pointed out. 'You're in it.' He scowled. 'Why don't you use your body?' said Eithe, her mouth full of crunch and red slime.

'None of your business,' said the Mirror Man.

Eithe sucked the cracker crumbs from her lips and stuck her finger into the jar to scrape at the last of her sauce. She licked it with relish. 'I saw you fall,' she said.

'Yes,' he said. He seemed taken aback by her sudden interest, as though he hadn't expected her to show concern.

'Did it hurt?'

'No. I'm further away from it.'

There was something sad about the unfeeling way he spoke about his own body.

'Is it strange, being in the television?' she asked. 'Do you feel famous?'

'I feel flat.'

She laughed, and the stretch of her jaw turned into a yawn, the pink skin at the back of her throat spasming. 'Oh God,' she said, 'I need to rest.'

'We have things to discuss.'

'After I shower and sleep.'

The Mirror Man grumbled impotently.

Eithe found the master bedroom. The mattress was as high as her hip and copies of the *Wall Street Journal* and *Business* lay on the bedside table. The bed linen was purple Egyptian cotton. 'Swanky,' she said, and went into the bathroom. Eithe, unfamiliar with luxury, felt the towels, fascinated by their softness, and ran the hot water right to the top of the bath. Every lotion and bath oil she could find went in, until the surface of the water was thick with botanicals, green tea essence and jojoba.

'Wait,' she said, her fingers playing with the wool of her tatty jumper. 'You can see me out of every reflection, right?'

'Yes,' he said, from the mirror.

'Can't you shut your eyes? I'm going to strip off.'

The Mirror Man didn't reply, but she was already pulling at the zip of her jeans. Her briefs and bra hit the mat and there was a slosh as she stepped into the bath. 'It's okay now,' she said, submerged up to her neck in bubbles. Then a thought hit her. 'You can look out of the loo as well,' she said.

'Eithe, I'm not really concerned about your, er, undercarriage,' he said.

'You can though, can't you?'

'Yes,' he said, 'but the last thing I want to do is look up your—'

'We'll have to work out a system,' she said. 'I could turn the light off before I sit down.'

'I'll close my eyes,' he said, reluctantly. Eithe didn't trust him. She even took off the cheap little ring that cinched her finger because the paste gemstones winked and shone. She wrapped herself in a towel and padded back to the bed. She slipped beneath the hand-stitched quilt and closed her eyes. The Mirror Man regarded her dispassionately.

She muttered and moved, her limbs twitching as if she was ridden by an unpleasant dream. The Mirror Man didn't wake her. It was not his job to comfort this strange girl, who seemed too young to be living in her own body.

Eithe woke suddenly and called for help, but only a croak escaped. For a second, she sat silent, her heart beating so fast it hurt. Her eyes adjusted to the gloom. It was still night-time. The only movement was the glow and fade of headlights, sliced into tiger stripes by the window blinds. She wanted to knock on her dad's door and shiveringly curl up at the foot of his futon. She wanted to cuddle a night-time teddy. She wanted her mother. But that was impossible, so she closed her eyes and pretended that she wasn't afraid.

In the morning, she was face down with the covers kicked-off. There were bruises in the region of her kidneys, but if the Mirror Man saw them, he said nothing.

She showered with the shower curtain closed, oblivious to the reflection in each tiny droplet. Breakfast was coffee, taken strong with sugar and no milk. There was no kettle, and the Mirror Man grudgingly explained how to use the complicated espresso machine.

'It's not FairTrade,' said Eithe.

'Who gives a damn,' said the Mirror Man. It was not a question.

If Eithe had been Joe, she would have shouted, 'Me and the barefoot pickers!' but she wasn't, so she didn't.

'It's high-grade Arabica and it'll wake you up. Get it down you.'

The fridge and the cunningly seamless cupboards were bare, so the coffee lay like a black lake in her empty stomach. 'If I was mad,' said Eithe into the mug, 'would I be able to tell the difference between my dreams and reality?'

'If you are mad, then it is a shared nightmare,' said the Mirror Man from the dregs. 'Now, about our enterprise. I would like you to search my apartment. There might be a clue somewhere. Maybe we'll find out who I am. Start in the folders over there. Look for bills, letters, anything that will tell us who I am and where I've been.'

'But—' said Eithe.

'What else do you have to do? Where else can you go?'

Eithe's mouth moved into a straight line. She thought about her own flat, which was signed in her fiancé's name, and about her abandoned job in accounts. Her money was gone. 'Okay,' she said.

She went through drawers and cabinets, and though she found a lot of documents, they were all financial and told her nothing except that he was good at his job. The numbers that fed into his personal account ran in smooth curving lines, bulging with each bonus. They did not correlate with the diminishing business numbers, which dropped precipitously about five years into the record. She found cartons of cigarettes secreted away in a neat stack in a cupboard.

'Just shut the door,' said the Mirror Man, wearily. 'You don't know how horrible it is to crave something you can't have.'

The only thing she discovered that looked personal, and therefore out of place, was a small box beneath the bed. It was a biscuit tin, and the lid was wedged on tight. She struggled to open it with her quick-bitten fingers, and when she did, the things inside exploded onto the quilt.

There were football cards featuring Beckham, Owen and Rooney, ticket stubs for rock gigs, a receipt for a visit to Thorpe park, a tiny toy racing car, a photograph of a little boy standing on sand clutching a plastic stegosaurus, and, most tragically of all, a green plush dinosaur, its head hanging from a loose neck, the stuffing squeezed by the cuddling hands of a young child. There was also a soft-cover diary, stained and battered.

'Wow, you really liked dinosaurs,' said Eithe. There was no response. 'This is all old,' she continued, sorting through. 'The stubs are dated from years ago.'

'Rubbish,' said the Mirror Man, his words coming metallic from the stippled lid. 'All of it.'

'Wait a moment,' said Eithe. 'There's this. It doesn't look like the rest.' She opened the diary. On the first page, someone had glued a small, rainbow-striped card.

'It isn't a journal. It's a scrapbook. This is a place in Montmartre,' said Eithe. 'This is from somewhere in Germany – Würzburg, and more, Italy, Greece...' Her head snapped round as her phone rang. She froze.

'Do you want to get that?'

Eithe brought the ancient handset out. This phone call was from Joe. She considered ignoring it, just as she'd ignored all the calls from work.

'God, that's huge,' said the Mirror Man. 'You could throw it in the swimming pool and force kids in pyjamas to jump in after it for personal survival training. Except they wouldn't be able to lift it so they'd probably drown.'

The happy little tune shrilled like tinnitus. The rush and current of her blood synchronised with the sound. 'Go on,' said the Mirror Man. 'It might be important.' Her hands were unsteady as she accepted the call and sat, ear to ear, with the Mirror Man.

'Eithe,' said Joe, his voice raw and ragged with passion. 'Eithe, where are you? I've been out looking for you for two days.'

'Away.'

'Who did you go out with? Was it the girl from work?'

'Maybe.'

'Did you drink? Are you with another man?'

'Perhaps.'

'Who is he?'

'I don't know.'

The timbre of Joe's voice shifted to a low growl.

'Did he rape you?'

'What?' said Eithe.

'If it was rape, then it wasn't your fault. I'll forgive you. Did you say no?'

Eithe cut the call.

She leaned against the bed and sucked in a
shuddering breath.

The phone rang again.

'The signal went,' said Joe. 'Are you all right?
What happened?'

'I don't know.'

'Tell me where you are and I'll come and get you.'

'I'm not sure—'

There was a very long pause.

Eithe recognised the tone, because she'd heard it before.
The voice wanted to reach through the phone, clamp its
hand around her neck and crush her windpipe.

'You're not sure?' he said.

'Please, Joe—'

'You went out, against my wishes, and you're not sure if
you want to come back?'

'But—'

The phone went dead and Eithe let it go. It dropped
with a dull thump and lay in the carpet like a great black
beetle. 'He sounds lovely,' said the Mirror Man, tinny
through the mouthpiece. Eithe was too shaken to reply.
The black beetle bucked on the floor as a text message
arrived. Eithe opened it.

I am coming for you.

She shut it again. She sat on the carpet, unmoving,
her arms wrapped around her long legs. She felt small
and scared.

'He'll find me,' she said. 'Oh, he'll find me. I had two
things in the world I was sure about, and one of them
was him.'

'So?'

'He wants me back.'

'You don't want go back.'

She gnawed on a knuckle.

'Your problem,' she said. 'Maybe we could find a doctor.'

The Mirror Man failed to repress a scornful laugh.

'Yes,' he said. 'Because of course there's a diagnosis for what I'm suffering from. A non-terminal loss of body.'

Eithe was hurt.

'I need you to go to the address on the card. Hurry,' said the Mirror Man. 'I don't have the luxury of time. Look, Eithe, I'll pay your expenses. All of them. You can get some nice clothes. Okay, not clothes then,' he backtracked when he saw her expression. 'If clothes aren't your thing. What is your thing? I can help you buy it.'

Her eyes narrowed with suspicion, but he continued.

'He stole your money,' he said. 'He's using it to get you. And he didn't think twice. I'm offering you an escape. You take me where I want to go and I'll pay your expenses.'

'You want to go abroad. I've never been abroad. Yes,' she said. 'Yes, I'll go.'

'Good. I'll give you my passwords. You can make the transfer online. There's a computer in the other room. And while you're at it, email the hostel and book a bed.'

They couldn't shake on the agreement, but later, in the living room she put her hands flat on the shiny black coffee table and he matched them, palm to palm.

The Trail

SOMEONE WAS BANGING ON THE door.

Joe dragged himself out from under the duvet, knees aching with inaction, and answered the knocking knuckles.

Louse stood in the corridor, small and bedraggled, her dreadlocks stale with old rain. Her clothes were a mismatch of home-stitched scraps, charity-shop chic and organic woollen-wear. Unlike Eithe, she wore her second-hand apparel as a statement, customised with appliquéd patches bearing the WWF panda, the CND logo, little messages like YOLO (You Only Live Once) and We Are The 99%.

'What?' said Joe.

They'd met at the short-lived Occupy Manchester movement when a policeman stopped to frisk Louse, who was wearing a V for Vendetta mask identical to one that had been used two weeks before by a mugger in Moss Side. Joe had intervened and been arrested for his trouble. After that, the girl had become as stubbornly adherent as her namesake.

'What are you doing?' she asked.

'Waiting.'

'You're better off without her,' she said, after wrinkling her nose at the smell. 'She was a colossal drip.'

Joe knew that. He'd thought that she would always stay, because she would never be able to make up her mind to leave. Her running shook him to the core.

'Why are you eating Dominos?' asked Louse. 'They're full of crap and the salami is probably reformed. Maybe it's factory farmed.'

'Go away, Louse,' he said, but she shook her head.

'A bunch of us are going on the march tomorrow,' she said. 'You'll come, won't you?'

Her grey eyes were wide and earnest.

Joe wanted to join the march. He'd been waiting for it all year, planning for it and thinking up slogans, and he'd spent hours putting together the banner. He intended to walk with his people, with the disenfranchised and dispossessed, with the redundant, with the families who lost their houses when the market crashed and with the teachers whose pensions had been stolen.

He wished to show solidarity with the disabled folk whose housing benefits were cut even though they were missing limbs and needed the extra room for their equipment, with the nurses from closing wards, with the social workers crushed by their caseloads. He would have stood shoulder to shoulder with the students who were thousands of pounds in debt and would remain so for decades. He was with the jobseekers, seeking where no jobs could be found – two-and-a-half-million people scrabbling for four-hundred-thousand places.

He wanted to march against the bankers and businessmen and selfish speculators and the politicians who had sat in their plush studies and central London penthouses and let it go on, who had let the system age and warp because it didn't matter if it broke and haemorrhaged, drowning the poor, just so long as the invisible stream of noughts, numbers and hypothetical gold kept pooling in the right places.

But he wanted to find Eithe more; he wanted to see confusion spread over her face. He wanted to pin her down and watch her try to crawl away in ten different directions at once.

'No,' he said, and slammed the door.

He lurched into the lounge, fired up the ancient computer and navigated to Eithe's email inbox. His reflection blurred on the matt screen. When it asked him to enter a password, he paused. Inside, he felt like clockwork, like an algorithm, like tumbling dice, like a ball spinning in a roulette table, unknowable but predetermined.

He opted for: answer the secret question: Who is your favourite artist?

Carefully, he typed out his guess. I--don't--know. He waited for one interminable second. Then the screen read: Welcome back, Eithe. His hands shook as he opened her emails. There was an old message in the first folder from Imai, Gem. It read:

how about a hen nite, girlies? drinkahol and fit man–strippers, yeh?! lol.

'Got you,' he said.

At the End of
the Rainbow

EI THE SAT BACK ON THE grey Eurostar cushions, closed her eyes and tried to loosen her muscles. The world went fuzzy as the engine shifted gear.

'Your card,' she said. 'It has a name on it. Casey Jones. Is that you?'

'No. But it's not someone else, if that's what you're worried about. In my line, I suppose it paid to have an emergency stand-by.'

She faced the window. In the reflection, he was sitting in her seat. She picked at the calloused skin under her bitten nails but he tapped his foot, a movement that jarred her nerves. The train was going fast, but not fast enough. She didn't want to see the black outside the window – she wanted to go past the speed of dark. Then perhaps she would feel better

Billions of gallons of salt water sloshed somewhere above the vastness of rock. In the end, the tiredness of a disturbed night and the ebb of adrenaline took Eithe and her head drooped against its rest. Submerged in exhaustion, she did not wake until Paris.

She stepped from the train with a sticky face and a brain full of fluff.

The *Gare du Nord*, with its confusion of French signage and babble of accents, was a blur to Eithe. The Mirror Man raged and chafed, gesturing from every surface as she meandered from the platform, moving with a kind of slow wonderment.

'Hurry up,' he mouthed, but she wasn't aware of him. The Metro didn't tell her to 'mind the gap', and it didn't stop before the doors unlocked so she found herself stepping from the moving carriage.

She arrived at Montmartre and emerged into a miasma of fine drizzle, which veneered the shutters and flecked the parked mopeds. The Mirror Man was present in the shop windows as her soles slapped the steep cobbled pavement, but she stared fixedly ahead. By the time she wandered past the edifice of the Sacre Coeur, she was out of breath. Gargoyles goggled down at her and she would have shivered if it hadn't been for the bird shit that slid down between their ears and took away some of their menace.

Eithe stopped and looked down over Paris, which glittered and smoked under a hazy honey sky. Vertigo stole over her. Her phone jiggled and beeped in her pocket, and she pulled it free, but stood staring out over the metropolis.

A text arrived. It read:

I still love you. I haven't cancelled the wedding.

Eithe's expression was grim.

'Well,' the Mirror Man muttered. 'If money won't make you move, maybe he will.'

Eithe hadn't heard him, but there was some truth to his words. She followed the slope until she came to a busy road where the flow of traffic obeyed no rules that she could see. The hostel nestled in a residential terrace. Someone had painted the front wall with a rainbow. The colours were faded. The door in the indigo stripe was unlocked, admitting Eithe into a warm space with an aroma of fresh laundry and well-travelled living bodies. The waiting receptionist looked elegant and tired. She breathed deeply down her tapered nose.

'Can I help you?' The voice was accented lightly, in the same way that an after-note of her perfume accented the air of the room.

'I emailed about a room. Do you have one available?'

'Name?'

'Eithe.'

'Ah, we do. Was it to be dorm, double or single?'

'Double,' said Eithe automatically.

The receptionist turned to look through the records and Eithe glanced around.

There were soft sofas tucked against the walls. There was a pin-perforated cork board holding pictures of smiling travellers. Eithe shifted her feet on the unvarnished floorboards, which creaked. The building was busy, but it looked battered, as though it was being cared for and repaired by someone without much money. The receptionist flexed her louche fingers on the keyboard.

'Yes,' she sighed. 'We do have a room for you.'

She considered Eithe through her eyelashes, leaned forward and slid a key across the desk. Two exhausted girls walked in from the street. They wilted against each other, their fingers twined together. If one moved, the other would fall.

'Okay,' said Eithe.

'The shower is en-suite. Check-out is at ten o'clock. This is a no smoking establishment. The kitchen is open for breakfast after eight thirty.'

'Thank you. *Merci*. Um. Thanks.'

'I'm Juliette. It means youthful.' Her voice was smoky with irony.

'I'm Eithe. It was a mistake.'

'Good to meet you. Now excuse me.'

Eithe found her room and threw the bag onto her bed. The walls were thick, but footsteps filtered through and so did raised voices and the scuffing of furniture on the floor. Outside, weighty yellow clouds recycled the city glow.

A sense of hugeness hit her in the space below her breastbone and made her ache. That wasn't a home sky. It was a French sky. The light that was shining on the wet road was not light that had fallen on her childhood garden, or slid through the windows of her little flat. A ribbon of grey water lay between her and everything she knew.

'Why didn't you ask her?' said the Mirror Man, impatiently.

'I'm tired,' said Eithe.

She pulled the blind down and returned to the bed. Her buttocks hit the mattress and her shoulders dipped. She sat still for a while. Then she rubbed her burning eyes, sniffled the snot back up her reddened nose, woke her phone and dialled.

'Are you calling your boyfriend?' said the Mirror Man, but she did not respond. A woman's voice came out of the receiver, concerned and reedy.

'Eithe?'

'Gem?'

'I was wondering how you were. No one knew where you got to. We thought you'd fallen into a ditch or something on the way home.'

'I'm okay.'

'Oh good.' The relief was genuine. 'The boss was asking when you'll be back in. He's not happy. He said he'd been calling your house phone all day.'

'I don't know when I'll be back,' said Eithe. 'Sorry.'

'You sound like you're talking through a colander. Is the reception bad where you are?'

'I'm in Paris,' said Eithe, 'on my own. Sort of.' She giggled, once, sharply, with the absurdity of it. There was a tinge of hysteria to the sound.

'All right,' said Gemma, slowly. 'Why?'

'I can't really tell you that.'

'Are you okay? Will you be coming back?'

'I don't know. I'm leaving. Can you just tell them that? Don't tell them where I am. Please.'

'Will do,' said Gemma. 'Take care, darling. We miss you, babes.'

Eithe put the phone away and lay down.

'Hey,' said the Mirror Man. 'Hey! Wakey-wakey.'

'Do you remember this place?' she said, eventually.

'I do,' said the Mirror Man. 'But not why I was here.'

'Something to do with money?'

'What makes you say that?'

'I saw your documents. I do numbers,' said Eithe.

He shrugged.

Eithe shambled into the bathroom to scrub her face. 'How did you enter the glass?' she said.

'If I knew that, I'd know how to get out.'

She lifted her hand and ran her fingers across her bland features. 'It's so strange not to see myself,' she said to the cracked bathroom mirror. 'You don't even move like me.'

'Well, get a move on and set me free.'

Eithe gave him a blank look. 'Why do you need me?' she said. 'Why can't you look yourself?'

'I don't have to justify myself to you,' said the Mirror Man. 'Go and ask the receptionist if she has any info.'

'You're going to have to stop ordering me around at some point,' said Eithe, but she obeyed.

The receptionist's teeth were very white against her red lipstick. Fine lines bunched and radiated out around her moving mouth. 'Did you find the room to your satisfaction?' she said. Eithe's eyes were drawn to a corn-gold strand stuck to the receptionist's lip-gloss. The rest of Juliette's hair was dusted with grey.

'Yes, thanks.'

'Ah,' said the Frenchwoman. 'If you need anything then you must ask. How do you like our hostel?'

'I don't have much to compare it to.'

Juliette looked over Eithe's shoulder at the mirror mounted on the back wall, and for an instant, she met the Mirror Man's eyes unwaveringly. Her look was one of speculation.

'One moment. *Bonjour messieurs*,' she said as two men shouldered through the door. They were laden with heavy bags. As the receptionist signed them in, they shared a quiet kiss. Eithe felt her face flare.

'You did not know,' said Juliette, 'what it is to be a rainbow hotel? My partner and I, we opened it. *C'est bien.* It is good.' She smiled for the first time. It was a slow, slinking thing. 'Sweet,' she said, at Eithe's confusion, at her naivety. 'Tonight,' she said. 'I think you should dine with me. Forget the tourist menus. I will show you real cuisine.'

7

Breaking

GEMMA FROM THE OFFICE LOOKED immaculate in a mini dress as she stood in front of the mirror with a glass of fizzing wine. She was expecting a nice meal at Petrus, and she was dressed in something shapely and tasteful. She raised the glass in salute to the late, great Alexander McQueen, as she always did when she wore her favourite outfit, drained the wine and selected an eye shadow to bring out the depth of her brown irises. She expertly dusted one ivory-skinned, unfolded lid.

When her phone went off, she hooked it between her shoulder and chin to continue her careful application.

'Oh hi! How are you? Me? Drunk? Of course. I have a drinking problem,' she said drily, regarding her empty glass. 'I've run out of wine.

'Yes, I've got a few minutes till they pick me up, don't worry. Oh, no. Not tonight. No, that was a rare one. I'd hoped she would, but she hasn't been back to the office since. To be honest, it's about time she took a few days off. I've never known her take a holiday. A bit of me hopes she's just decided to pick up and leave. God knows I want to do that sometimes.

'Yeah. Yeah, she's quite shy. Well, she got talking a bit more at the bar. Dad from Haiti apparently, but she said she didn't know any more. I know! Haiti! Think of all the stories he could tell. Oh yes?' She replaced the eye shadow, picked up a hairbrush and ran it through her sheer, black hair and juggled the handset to the other ear. She laughed once.

'I live in hope,' she said. 'But you know I like my men like I like my coffee, dark, strong and bitter.' The intercom buzzed.

'Really? Right. Look, darling, I have to go. That's them, I think, to pick me up. I'm not quite ready still. Yeah, you too. I'll see you on Monday. See you. Bye!'

She dropped her phone in her handbag and turned to the intercom.

'Hello?' she said. 'You're early.'

'No I'm not.'

She was taken aback. It was a man's voice.

'Who is this?'

'It's Joe. Joe King. I'd like to talk.'

Gemma recoiled. This was awkward. She knew about the argument, because Eithe, the quiet girl in accounts, told her about it after they'd had a few cocktails. It was the most she'd ever spoken before. She did not know Joe well. On the few occasions she met him at work functions, and once when she'd invited them to a house party, she'd noted him as mildly good looking with rolls of blond hair and the long features of a gravestone angel. He was never far from his fiancée.

Her spine tingled a warning, but the champagne interfered with the signal.

'It isn't a good time,' she said.

'Please,' he begged. 'I won't stay long. I don't know where she is, and I'm worried about her.'

She felt a bit sorry for him, so she let him in.

'Hello—' she began, her hand still on the doorknob.

He was dishevelled; his hair awry and his eyes were bloodshot. His clothes gave off a stench of stale sweat. She remembered now that he was very tall. When he stood next to Eithe, it was less obvious, but he towered over Gemma.

'Have you been drinking?' she asked. She tried to close the door, but his foot was already jammed in the frame. Joe shouldered through the gap. It was not a gentle push and she was wearing heels. The air blasted from her lungs.

'Do you know where she is?' Joe asked.

Gemma was shocked, but she was not afraid, not yet. The Joe she'd met before was a sweet, rather earnest man, who wore his ethics on his sleeve. She believed he was drunk and distressed and not entirely himself. After a bath, a nap and a chat, he would be fine. She didn't know that this boy, with his hair sticking out and his patchy jumper, wanted so much to be taken seriously by somebody, by anybody, that he was prepared to hunt a woman as far as she would go. It didn't occur to her that she was in danger.

She followed Joe into her lounge. 'Please,' she said. 'I'm going out and I have to get ready.'

'What happened?' he said. 'You should know. It was your idea to go out without me. She just said okay, didn't she? Did she go home with him? Did you see them kissing? What did he look like?'

'Look honey, I'm not into threesomes,' Gemma snorted. 'So if something did happen, I wasn't there.'

It was the laugh that did it. She saw his eyes change.

Gemma's flat was simple. There wasn't much to break, but she did have a geode resting on the mantelpiece of the feature fireplace. It was as big as a cat skull and the colour of milk. Joe picked it up and slammed it into Gemma's face. While she lay on the floor, bleeding from her nose, he leant over her and said, 'Where is she?'

'I don't know,' she sobbed. He seemed gratified. At last, someone was taking him seriously.

'Did she tell you?'

'Tell me what?' she said, the syllables punctuated by frightened gasps. She was playing for time, so he kicked her in the gut.

'Where she is.'

The man panted, with the dripping stone in his hand. Her mind turned over unevenly because of the concussion. Eithe was in Paris. She knew that. But she wouldn't tell him. 'Listen, you idiot. We're not,' she said, leaking red spit, 'exactly BFFs. She just sits across from me. I only thought she needed a night out. Just once.'

He left her bleeding on the floor. She watched him through swelling flesh as he scrabbled through her stuff, emptying drawers, thrusting sheaves of paperwork onto the floor, sweeping lipsticks and perfume from the vanity cabinet, until he found her phone in her bag.

She was scared now, so she said nothing.

'Call her,' he said. 'Call her. Say you're calling from work. They want to know where she's gone, or she'll be sacked.' He forced the phone into her twitching hand. 'Do it, you stupid bitch.'

She looked up at him, blood pooling in the white of one eye.

'I don't know, Joe. The signal here is pretty rubbish—'

She was upsetting him so he punched her to sleep.

Gemma's flat was simple. There wasn't much to break, but he broke it anyway. He did not notice the dark thing slip from beneath the unconscious girl and gather beneath his soles.

Reve a Deux

THE FRENCHWOMAN'S QUARTERS WERE IN an attic room. She was waiting at the door.

'With your leave,' said Juliette, and she leaned in. For a moment, Eithe thought the Frenchwoman was administering a continental kiss from cheek to cheek, and she stood stock-still, waiting for it to be over. But instead she felt the press of lips against hers, and a faint taste of clean tobacco and the tip of a tongue. Then Juliette stood back.

'Ah,' she said. 'I see. So it is that.'

Eithe fought the urge to wipe the back of her hand across her mouth. 'I'm not—'

'No,' said Juliette. 'I am sorry. You are not. Forgive me. When I saw your reflection, I saw – for a moment I thought that you had a man's soul in a woman's body, and I was intrigued. But there is nothing. Nothing at all. No desire, no repugnance. I do not know what you are. I think perhaps you do not, either.'

'I'll go,' said Eithe. 'I—'

'No, no,' said Juliette. 'I meant no offence. Please, sit. I have the food waiting. It was not my intent to seduce you. Only to know you more.'

'Eithe, sit down,' said the Mirror Man. 'She might have information.'

Juliette lifted an eyebrow and cocked her head.

'Will you come in?'

The Mirror Man said, 'Ask her if she remembers me at all?'

Eithe said, 'I'm trying to find out if there's a man in your database. He would have stayed here about ten, fifteen years ago. He was about six foot tall, dark hair, a bit…'

Juliette frowned. 'So many people pass through our doors. Eithe, *chère*, sit, sit. And tell me why you are here.'

As Juliette busied herself at the stove, Eithe told the Frenchwoman an abbreviated version of her story. She mentioned Joe, but not the bruises, and she didn't mention the Mirror Man, yet.

'I just needed to get away,' she said, as the clouds darkened through the skylight. There were three seats at the table. Juliette placed an embroidered cushion on the third and rested a violin gently on the cloth, propping it against the backrest. The wood was faded but polished to a high shine, allowing a faint version of Mirror Man to watch from it, his face made cartoonish by the curves. A small dog, all shaggy fur, put its front paws on the chair and thrust its blunt nose at the wood. 'It's a footstool with a face,' said the Mirror Man. He rubbed at the nasal smudge from the inside but it didn't fade.

Juliette lifted the lid from a dish. Six glossy snail shells sat on a bed of lettuce. There was a puddle of butter in each one. A spindly fork sat on her serviette. It had two slender tines. Eithe looked at it with consternation. 'It's an acquired taste, but it isn't nasty at all,' said the Mirror Man.

'Really?' said Eithe weakly as she rummaged. Her wrist movement felt clumsy rather than subtle. She found herself staring at a curl of grey flesh on the end of the fork. She blanched but forced her mouth open. She put the snail on her tongue. The taste of salt butter and heat-softened garlic flowed down her throat. She chewed and she swallowed. Then she nodded.

Juliette smiled, and this time it was genuine. 'It's surprising to find out what you like, sometimes. Unexpected things can have a delectable taste.' She cleared the plates and returned to the table with a thick brown casserole.

The Mirror Man stared from the edge of reality, the taste buds of his absent tongue redundant, his nostrils defunct. Eithe met his envious stare in the empty plates and cutlery. 'This smells gorgeous,' she said and for a little while, all that could be heard was the scratching of metal on china. The dog woke up and circled the table, its frantic nub of a tail wagging.

'This is nice,' said the Mirror Man, with a bright, rictus grin. 'Isn't this nice? Who the hell am I?'

Juliette picked up a piece of beef and dropped it for the begging dog. He caught and swallowed it and licked the grease from his moustache. 'Schnuff,' said the dog, and Juliette made room for it on her lap.

'There's another man,' said Eithe. 'I'm trying to find him. I think he stayed here. Is there any way we can check?'

'You are a strange girl,' said Juliette, but the words were not unkind. 'I do not think you know yourself yet. There are some people who are born whole, and there are others that build themselves. There is a third type who realise who they are all in a moment. I did not know what it was I wanted in life until I met my partner and then it was all clear as,' she rang her fingernail against the rim of the wine glass.

Eithe nodded, uncomprehending. 'What a load of bollocks,' said the Mirror Man. 'What did you mean about my reflection?' said Eithe, who still half-thought she'd imagined her companion. 'You said about a male soul.' She saw the Mirror Man lean forward in every reflection.

'It is nothing,' said Juliette. 'Only something I saw from the side of my eye. I think sometimes some of us do not really fit in ourselves. Our minds and our bodies do not always match, or our outside is not like our inside. What we are does not necessarily sit well with what we could be or what others expect to see.

'It interests me, these little signs, these clues that you can sometimes see, not in the face or in the body, but, perhaps, in the shadows behind them. Do you understand?'

'Not really,' said the Mirror Man, but Juliette seemed to reply to him, even though she couldn't see him and didn't hear him.

'There is a French word, *bardache*, that was taken to describe people of the First Nations in America who did not fit what western people thought was their seeming role. It is not a good word. Now they call us *two spirits*, which is a kinder way of saying a woman who also has some of the qualities of a man, or a man who has some of the qualities of a woman, or someone who is neither or both. I thought for a moment I was seeing your male soul. It would not be the first time. Then I blinked and he was gone.'

Eithe looked at the violin, which lounged on the chair, all polished brown curves and long neck.

'Your partner,' she said. 'You don't mean a business partner, do you?'

'Where is she?'

Juliette rested her hand on the little dog. 'I first saw her across the street as she unfolded her manuscript, lifted the violin and set it to her chin. The body of the instrument is supposed to be a woman, with a pinch-waist, round-rear and long-drawn moaning music. We smiled at each other.

'She came to Paris to escape her mother, who wanted little footprints and finger paintings. But back then, to have children you also had to have a man. Her mother smothered her so she picked up the instrument and left.

'She had hair the colour of seasoned wood worn pale by playing. Her name was a waltz: Romilly. She was fire and I was ice. When we came together, we made liquid. I still know the shape of her better than I know my own.'

Eithe nodded. She knew Joe better than she knew herself.

'Love is not always easy. I remember my father telling me it was against God's will; that we were doing something sinful and dirty. But we were not. After the *jouissance*, and *la petite mort*, there was no mess. We just licked our fingers and washed our faces clean.

'My *grand-maman* died, and we went to the funeral. My family stood in black and made a fence of their

shoulders and spines. The coffin went down into the
ground as they said the mass. Beside me Romilly stood
tall, detached from them, with her dust-to-dust dry
eyes. They would not let me lay a flower by the grave.
Afterwards, my brother came up to us. I smiled. I thought,
one at least will talk to us. And then he spat. His gunk
slid down my face. When we went back to our cheap little
room, Romilly played violin until her fingers blistered and
I begged her to stop.'

For the first time, the Frenchwoman's composure broke.
Her voice wobbled.

'But there were good times?' said Eithe.

'Oh yes,' said Juliette. 'In Paris, we went to the top of
the Eiffel tower. She was afraid of heights, but with me
she could look down to the ground. We laughed together
at the woman who married the tower after falling in love
with it. When she spoke of it, it was as a wife talks about
a strong, tall husband, and even though it was just metal
and architecture, she thought it had a soul that could speak
with hers. There are far stranger than we in the world.
Where there are people, there are infinite possibilities.

'One night we sat in our little apartment and discussed
how we had no family but each other, no place but our
tiny home, and we thought about how many others were
suffering the same, how many young people were cast out,
how many people were being punished for the crime of
their right, real love. And we thought; if we cannot keep
our family, then we can make one for ourselves and for all
those others who cannot.

'We took out loans and made our future. When our
hostel was ready, we stood side by side and cut the pink
ribbon at the same time so that it fell in three pieces.
People applauded. Genet, a famous poet. came to stay here

in the first week, although he was old and angry. He visited the grave of Oscar Wilde in the *Père Lachaise*, and bowed to the tomb and rubbed away some of the lip-prints the younger ones leave on the stone.'

She sighed and passed her fingers across her forehead.

'She does well, our hostel, she has many friends. But we put ourselves in debt to buy her and I must employ more people. The hours I work are too long. I think perhaps we have three months, maybe four, before we must close our door. Then our dream will end.'

Eithe looked down at the lonely violin. The strings were frayed with age and there was dust on the fingerboard.

'She died,' she said. 'Didn't she?'

'Yes,' said Juliette. 'She became ill, and it spread hard lumps through her flesh. I believe it came from her mother, not through inheritance, but through the hate she sent down the phone and through her letters. We fought it, but the doctors put poison in her to stop the growth and she could not keep going. They would not let me lie with her as she died, because I was not legally her wife, nor she mine. Our president would not allow marriage between two women. So at home I laid my head beside where hers should have been and, when I woke and went to the hospital, I was told she was gone and only her body was left. I was not even allowed to say goodbye.

'Her mother tried to take the Rainbow away from me, claiming half belonged to her as next of kin, and took me to court. In the eyes of the law, we were business partners and no more. I had to settle. My parents would not speak with me. It was like a dagger in the heart. But Juliette is always left behind. And this time, she will go on, even without her Romilly.' She reached for the bottle. 'More wine?'

'No, thank you,' said Eithe.

'Ah,' said Juliette, as she upended the remains into her glass. 'All the more for me.' She shrugged. 'You learn that sometimes, there is a choice to be made. Between one misery and another. Between one happiness and another.'

'I know that already,' said the Mirror Man. 'Jesus. She just goes *on*.' Eithe sat, paralysed by his rudeness.

'I forgive them,' said Juliette. 'I gave up the fighting. You cannot have the *dialogue de sourds*. The two deaf people shouting. Now it is for them to forgive me.'

'Eithe please,' said the Mirror Man. 'We're wasting time.'

'I think we have to go,' said Eithe.

'What's the hurry?' said Juliette.

'I – I don't feel very well,' said the Mirror Man. 'There's a hundred miles of numbness and, on the other side of that, there's pain.'

'I'm being paid to be here,' said Eithe, to Juliette. 'I'm on a deadline. Sorry.'

'Come on, let's go,' said the Mirror Man.

'Okay,' Eithe said.

Juliette stood, deposing the little dog who landed on the floor in a huff. She ushered Eithe to the door. 'Thank you,' said the younger woman, as they paused, awkwardly, before the stairwell. This time, Juliette simply brushed against her cheekbones, one at a time.

As Eithe left, Juliette turned to the violin and said, 'A very unusual girl. Did you mark how she listened?' In the stillness of the flat, the strings thrummed.

As Eithe trod the wedges of the spiral staircase, she was pensive. She turned back the covers of her bed and climbed under the duvet. She thought about the nothing kiss. She thought about Joe, she thought about going home and she thought about running east. Her mind felt heavy, like a set of scales perpetually unbalanced. When she thought about Joe, the loss of future kisses, of cool arms around her, of spice and pale skin, she felt a spasm of suffering. She had spent time adoring Joe's nose, the flimsy bits of hair at the corner of his jaw that the razor never reached and the v-shaped scar on his temple where a stone hit him at a demonstration. She hoped if she tried hard to like the little parts, they would merge and she would suddenly, definitely, love the whole.

'Don't worry,' said the Mirror Man, who misinterpreted her discomfort. 'I wasn't watching you and Juliette. Well, not like that. As far as I'm concerned, a bird in the hand is better than two in the bush.' Eithe did not reply. 'We leave tomorrow,' he said.

She sniffled. 'Go away.'

'I can't,' he said, reluctantly. 'There is something holding me to you. And even if there wasn't, I would just snap back to wherever my body was, because I'm tied to it. Sometimes I can feel it pulling.'

'You've asked the wrong person for help,' said Eithe. 'Goodnight, Mirror Man.'

She pushed her face into the pillow. After a while, she spoke out of the dark. 'Will you watch over me?' she said dozily. 'Like you did last night?'

'I didn't watch you last night.'

'Sure, okay.' She rolled over, and counted back from a hundred. After a while her breathing slowed and the rise and fall of her chest deepened. Despite what he'd said, the Mirror Man watched her. Every so often she gave out a gentle snore, and then a series of twitches ran through her resting body.

In the morning, Eithe packed and checked the little scrapbook. It held a postcard of a ceiling fresco in a town called Würzburg. 'Is it a nice town?' she asked. The Mirror Man shrugged. 'You watched me again last night,' she said.

'I don't have any bones or meat to lie down. I can't fall asleep and I can't laze around dreaming like you, so what else am I going to do?' he snapped. 'There's only so many times you can count the cracks in the wall. *It's not about you.*'

When she settled the bill, Juliette took payment and folded the receipt with nimble hands. 'Thank you,' she said, and then she leaned over the desk. 'Sometimes you have to go back to go forward. Choose well. And know.'

'Know what?' said Eithe.

'Your mind. *Bon voyage,*' said Juliette, handing Eithe the receipt.

'Goodbye'

It was only later, as she sped out of the city on another train that Eithe unfolded the paper and found the ring. It was dark gold with a crucifix incised into it.

A scribbled note read: *Send me a message when you wish on this number. Also our email.*

Maman Juliette

9

Dreamembering

IN A ROOM HUNDREDS OF miles away, a man battled with his bedsheets.

In the disordered sludge of his sleeping mind, Gemma leaned out of the dark, her face a white Noh mask stretched in a grimace of pain.

'Hello Joe,' she said. Her breath was hot on his face. It smelled of acetone and anger. He shrank down into the mattress. The shadow of her nose cut sharp across his cheeks like the shadow of a sundial. He tried to say, 'It wasn't me,' but the words wouldn't come. He told himself he was dreaming.

'Really?' she asked, jerking her head so that her matted, brown-clotted hair flopped. 'Really? Are you sure about that?'

The room was sucking at her, grey and grainy. The walls moved like lungs, bunching and stretching. Hours trickled by, and Gemma just breathed, boiling his forehead and the bridge of his nose and drying up the jelly of his terrified eyes. The fear-cold coiled around his spine and somewhere the two temperatures met, and he cracked like glass under stress.

He bit his tongue, and that was what woke him up.

A low moan wound from his dry throat. He lay, his lungs heaving, but he could not stay still so he crawled out of the bed and returned to the computer. He stared at the screen, drawn and blue with the light from the monitor. He clicked, refresh, refresh, refresh. A tendon in his wrist twanged with repetitive strain. He didn't want to go back to sleep. He was a pacifist – hadn't he always been a pacifist? – but violence found him in the vulnerable hours.

The *I* newspaper lay at his elbow, opened like a cracked ribcage. There were two small images of Gemma-from-the-office, one a faded instagram of her grinning at the camera, the other an image released by the police as part of a witness appeal – her head depressing a hospital pillow, the side of her face the colour of an aubergine. Her parents had agreed to use the picture to show the world what had happened to their little girl. It was only a small article, sandwiched between a worrying dip in the Dow Jones index and details of how a county council in North Wales buried a report about child abuse some time back in the 1990s.

The Girl In A Coma headline made him feel sick every time he saw it. He wanted to be sick. He wanted to punish himself and purge, and he would, but not before he found Eithe, because it was their fate to be together.

It was raining outside, and the water drumming on the window made the streetlight scatter and woke an old memory. He opened his own account, created a fresh email and started typing.

Eithe,

Do you still remember how we met?

Do you remember the library? The librarian wouldn't let me take a book out without proof of identity.

I had my passport, but he was being such a cock.

'Are you joking? This is a joke,' he said.

I was so pissed off, but you were there, and I asked if you would take the books out for me. I noticed your name when you pushed your card over. I said, 'Hello Eithe.'

You said, 'You got it right. That's unusual.'

And I said, 'A lot of people think I'm joking.'

You didn't get it. You said, 'It can't be that bad.'

That was when I knew I could love you.

I said, 'No, actually, it is. My name. Joe King. I thought about changing it by deed poll once I hit eighteen, but by then I'd spent so long correcting people that I didn't want to give up.'

I knew I'd heard your name before. And you blushed as you gave me the books. I promised I wouldn't get you fined, but I returned them when they were overdue, and the prick on the front desk wouldn't let me pay Eithe Dord's debt. He said it was your card, your problem. But I wasn't angry, because that was when I remembered who you were, and I knew it didn't matter, because we'd meet again.

I put the exact change in a pocket in my wallet and carried it around with me for weeks. And then I saw you, with your

curly hair, standing out of the crowd because of how tall you
were. That was when I knew it was fate. And I went up to you
and gave you the money, and you were amazed, and I asked
you out for coffee. You said okay, and that's how it started.

Just okay. That's all you said.

Are you okay now?

He sent the email. Then he signed off and logged into
her account.

Joe wiped his hand across his scratchy skin. The
muscles in his cheeks strained as they pulled his lips back
in a smile with too much gum and too much tooth. With
deliberation, he opened up the Sent folder. There were two
new messages. One was from him, the other was not.

Dear Sir/Madam,

I would like to book a room at the Rainbow. Would it be
possible to email me your information?

Eithe

'So you've found what you want,' the shadow on his
headrest whispered.

Joe wheeled away from the desk and clapped his hands
over his ears in terror.

Overland

THE HIGH SPEED TRAIN WAS sleek and quiet. It was not peak time, so the carriage was almost empty. The Mirror Man had insisted on First Class, because even if Eithe didn't care about the leg room, he didn't want to have to look at the economy class passengers.

Eithe said to the window, 'Am I any closer to getting rid of you?'

'Hopefully.'

She started filling in a postcard, the train so smooth on the tracks it didn't disturb her skritchy handwriting.

Dear Juliette,

*Thank you so much for the meal and your kindness. I just
thought I'd tell you there was a ring wrapped up in the paper
you gave me, and I wanted to know if I should post it back. I
will arrive in Würzburg soon.*

Eithe.

'Why are you keeping in touch with her?' asked the Mirror
Man. 'She can't do anything else for me.' The vibration
distorted his voice into a low growl.

She said, 'Because she was kind to me. You look sort
of sick.'

He shook his gaunt head. 'Just bored. I'd like a beer.
You have one.'

'We – I don't drink,' she said.

'You did once,' he said.

'On my hen night,' she said, 'and look what happened.
Besides, I can't just use your money up.'

'Eithe, parked in a garage in London, there's a
customised anthracite black Mercedes-Benz SLS AMG
that goes from nought to sixty less than four seconds. I just
drove it on Saturdays. My apartment is on the top floor. It
has panoramic views of the city and you need a periscope
to navigate through the carpet, but I only ever slept there. I
have an Armani suit made out of the cocoons of murdered
silk worms, and I don't have a body to put it on.'

Eithe made a noise of revulsion.

'Order one and drink it for me,' he said.

'I don't know what.'

'You don't prefer one?'

'I've never had a preference.'

'Eithe, opinions are like arseholes. Everyone has one.'

'And they are best kept to yourself?' she said, hopefully.

'No,' said the Mirror Man. 'I mean if you don't vent it occasionally, you will explode. Choose something.'

Eithe's face took on an unusually stubborn cast.

'Do you know how to say 'please'?' she said.

'I'm not going to beg you to – oh, okay.' He said, exasperated. 'Please will you let me buy you a drink?'

'Okay.'

So when the waiter arrived, she ordered a tall frosty glass of weißbier. It ran like gold down her throat. 'I've never tasted anything like this before,' she said.

'You've never lived,' said the Mirror Man.

'Maybe not,' she said.

'Keep your voice down,' he said. 'They'll think you're talking to yourself.'

'I never even knew there was a world out here,' she said, her consonants softened by the beer. 'I don't know if I want to know.' Her shoulder blades lifted against the leather seat. 'I don't have anyone else,' said Eithe in a dull monotone. 'We were going to get married in white, both of us, because I was his first and he was mine. He wanted to have a family with me. He said we were destined to be together, that we added up, two halves of a whole. He was happy with me. He said I took him seriously.' She put her fists up to her face. Her spine twisted and her shoulders jerked. A horrible bubbling noise sluiced from between her fingers. 'And now I've destroyed all of that.

'I'm going to have another beer. Okay? Okay.'

She ordered another bottle and it consoled her as she drank.

The train bowled through broad, golden fields which spread to the horizon, rising and falling with the flow of the land. Birds sat in chattering clumps on the electric lines. 'So what are we looking for?' she said, as she wiped the froth from her top lip. 'If some of you is in the mirror and your body is back there?'

'Well I recall some things,' the Mirror Man admitted. 'But not others. I don't know my name. Or remember my childhood, my parents or my friends. If we find my name, that might help. I could Google myself. Perhaps there are pictures. They might help me remember who I was.'

'And find a way to get you back to your body.'

'Mmm,' he said.

'What happens if I don't find a way to stitch you back in?' she asked.

'I think I'm safe for now.'

'That wasn't an answer,' she said.

The Mirror Man studied her as she licked her lips. 'Okay,' he said. 'You are naïve, but you aren't stupid. I'll be honest with you. I don't know. Maybe I'll just carry on like this until we do find it.'

'Ugh, That's a horrible thought,' she said.

'Yeah.'

'I wonder what happened to my reflection?' she said. 'Do you think I've lost part of myself? Am I in there with you?'

'Er,' he said, evasively. 'Not exactly.'

She looked at him searchingly, but he wasn't giving anything away. 'So, what now?' she said.

'You're going to buy a new phone, one that's internet enabled.'

'I'll put my ring back on as well,' she said, 'so there will always be something you can look out of that's close to me. So you can speak to me whenever you want.'

'Good,' he said.

'What's it like?' she asked timidly. 'Where you are?'

'Out here,' he said. 'It's indescribable.'

'Is it grey?'

'It isn't anything. Imagine nothing going on forever.'

'I think I can.'

'No,' he said. 'You can't. It's like looking through glass except there's no sky behind it or water to catch the light and turn it blue. It isn't grey or white or black. It's no colour.'

'When I ask you to look away, is that what you see?'

'Yes.'

'It could drive you mad.'

'Yes.'

'I won't ask you to look away again.'

'Thank you,' he said, and she was surprised by how grateful he sounded.

'Tell me what you remember,' she said. 'About your life.'

'I can't think of much,' he said. 'I think my memories are left locked in my brain, wherever that is now. That scares me, because what are we, except memories written in grey jelly? When that's gone, we're just cells. And I'm not even that. I'm just a bundle of fears and wants.'

'You are more than that,' said Eithe. 'Think.'

'I remember the sound of shredding paper and the hum of a computer. I remember smelling correction fluid. I don't remember my parents, or my girlfriends, except in bits. Do you think that's strange?'

'No,' said Eithe.

The Mirror Man said, 'I've lost it all. But you are young. You probably don't know what it is like to lose someone.'

'Yes, I do.'

They rested for a few heartbeats, both savouring old pain like salt.

She retrieved the ring from her purse and slid it on to her finger and he occupied the facets of the oval-cut glass. A faint echo of her heartbeat throbbed through the metal band.

When the train passed into Mannheim, they found a shop selling smartphones. Eithe hovered over a Blackberry, until the Mirror Man said, 'No, not that one. Try a Samsung Galaxy or an iPhone.'

The operative on the till took the Mirror Man's card, but she had to give him a billing address. When she realised she didn't know it, she handed her own details over. The Mirror Man looked vaguely queasy as he followed Eithe on the bullet train.

'What's wrong with you?' she asked. 'Motion sickness?'

'No,' he said. 'My inner ear isn't here. It can't be that.'

On the next train, Eithe typed her postcard message into an email and sent it as an experiment. Then she stowed the handset in her pocket.

The Mirror Man followed it in to the warm, dark pouch before the phone began to idle. He began to push here and there, on the screen, but then it went dark. He rode the rest of the way in sullen silence.

The Eloquent Spectre

JOE LOOKED AT THE HOLE his body made in the light, aghast at the tapering of the waist and the ceaseless flickering of the fingers.

It stalked him across the pavement, talking all the time.

He'd blocked his ears with tissue as he fled the flat and bought earplugs when he was in the airport, but there was still a background buzzing at the periphery of his distressed concentration. Paris was supposed to be a rainy city, but the sun cut strong across the streets, making his shadow even sharper.

He grabbed a pastry at a corner shop and ate it without tasting it, staring at the dance of his disembodied hands written across a whitewashed wall. The fingers wrote a familiar pattern. Joe narrowed his eyes. His shadow was signing at him, and he recognised two phrases.

'Talk me,' it gestured. 'See me.' He blinked. 'See me.'

'Hallucinations don't sign,' he said.

The shadow's drooping shoulders lifted and it signed with new vigour. 'Listen.'

Joe took the wadded plug from his ears. 'British Sign Language,' he said.

'Yes,' said his shadow. 'My little brother is deaf. I've known it since I was five. When did you learn it? I've been trying to get your attention for two days.' It was Gemma's voice. It made him want to block his ears again, but it was too late for that. 'Funny,' she said. 'I don't remember what he looks like. Just that he's deaf.'

'Shut up,' he said.

'It's so lonely here. I can hear things, but I can't see anything except your silhouette. You're like – real, and nothing else is. It's all fog and grey veils.'

'I'm not listening,' he said.

'You didn't seem to understand all of it. Are you a bit rusty?' Joe did not respond. 'I like that you tried,' she said, 'even if you have forgotten some of it. You can always pick it up again. What's your name? I'm sorry I can't tell you mine. I don't know it right now. I'm glad I found you. It's very boring, wherever I am.'

For a moment, his heart beat like a hummingbird's, and a gulf opened up in his abdomen. She was haunting him. She'd died of her injuries, and she was going to follow him, wading through the ether, to exact her revenge. And then he realised she couldn't see him, and she didn't know who he was.

Joe balled up the wrapper and threw it in the bin. He was an environmentalist, or he had been, and he did not like litter.

'So where are we going?' she said. 'I'm coming with you. I'm not going off on my own again.' Joe strode on, his chin pulsing as he chewed on his own teeth.

'You seem familiar,' said Gemma. 'Have we met before, on the other side? It's all a bit blurry and far away. I try to remember, and sometimes I get close, but I can't quite reach it. It's like swimming underwater without air, and the faster you move, the more your energy just ebbs away and you fail.

'My head hurts,' she said. She laughed. 'I don't even have a head, but it still hurts. I've been totally amputated. Do you think I'm the phantom pain? How does that even happen? Where are we?'

'Paris,' said Joe, bemused by the relentlessness of the breathy, lung-less whisper, and of her bonhomie.

'It's nice to have a break from work though. I haven't had a holiday in years. France is nice. Are we going to go to the *Arc de Triomphe*? Or the cute little cafés. I'm not too bothered about the tourist traps. And I wouldn't be able to see them anyway. Maybe a concert would be better – I could appreciate that.'

'I'm not sightseeing,' said Joe.

'Why are you here? Pleasure or business?'

'I'm looking for someone.'

'Who?'

'My wife.'

The wraith skipped along aside him, swinging her arms. 'How romantic! I'm coming too,' she said.

'No,' said Joe.

'Oh go on,' said the shade, brightly. 'I'm your new travel companion. I can't carry your bags, but I can keep you company.'

'I don't want company.'

'It's too late. I'm stitched to you, like when Wendy darned Peter Pan's shadow back on to his feet. Soap didn't work sticking it on, and you'll need more than soap to remove me.' The shadow reached through his shoe and tickled his soles. It was like being teased by a ghost. 'You have no choice.'

Something about her selection of words stopped his protests. Joe hunched his shoulders as he tackled the hill. He wasn't far from the Rainbow.

Night Shift

WURZBURG WAS QUIET AT ELEVEN pm. Eithe was a little unsteady as she walked, her arm aching from pulling her case.

'Left here,' said the Mirror Man. 'And just down the street.'

The hostel reminded her of a secondary school, all concrete, big square windows and plywood. She pushed the swing doors open over the scuffed linoleum floor. A small brass hand bell sat on the reception sill. 'Hello,' she said to the young man on the other side of the hatch. He looked up from his crossword and absent-mindedly brushed back his sandy fringe.

'*Guten tag*,' he said.

Eithe peered past the desk, into the little cubby-hole which held a bunkbed, a desk and a fridge. Empty mugs congregated on every surface. 'Are you on a long shift?' she asked, aware that she was still slightly tipsy. He looked up at her, his finger poised to turn a page.

'*Ja.* Until I finish the books.'

Eithe noticed that when he spoke, a dimple glimmered on his cheek. It disappeared when he turned back to the book. She liked the click-clacking of his consonants. The Mirror Man gurned out of a mug at her.

'Room three,' said the receptionist. 'It is a dormitory. Your key.'

'Ask him about the records,' said the Mirror Man.

'Um,' said Eithe.

'Here,' he disappeared below the desk and resurfaced with an armful of white bedding. '*Schwupp!*' he said as he dropped it into her waiting arms. 'There you are. *Guten nacht.*'

They stared at each other. Eithe felt something tickle in her stomach. She looked at his shoulders and at his clean, broad features, recognised his handsomeness and then she folded the thought away. 'Er, good night,' she said, blushing. She was ruffled as she found room three and went into the windowless cubicle bathroom. She hummed happily.

'You like him, don't you?' said the Mirror Man.

'Stop making faces at me when I'm with other people,' she said

'He didn't see me,' he said.

'You don't have to close your eyes, but can you look away?' she said to the mirror as she fiddled with the button of her jeans. 'I'm going to go to the toilet.' He obeyed, but she still breathed in sharply when she went back to the mirror. 'It's uncanny,' she said. 'Not seeing myself.'

'I know,' he said. 'There's not much I can do about it.'

'You're angry,' she said.

'I'm not used to it,' he said. 'I think whatever I was before I fell into the mirror, I had power.'

'You are quite selfish.'

'I just know what I want and how to get it. Take every opportunity, pass nothing up. Be the best you can be. The strong survive, the weak don't thrive. The world gives you nothing for free. You have to take it. Adapt or die.'

'That's your choice.'

'It's an obvious choice.'

'Even if you hurt other people? What about what they want?'

The Mirror Man said, "I am not other people. Therefore I can't be responsible for what they want.' Eithe was ready to reply, but a group of travellers arrived and filled the room with chatter.

All night, people came in and out of the dormitory, dumped bags and climbed the bunk bed ladders. She slipped into a slumber thick with dreams, the new phone on the pillow. As she slept, the Mirror Man pushed at the invisible barrier like a bee buzzing against a window, trying over and over to unlock the screen. But he couldn't marshal enough strength to press, to change something in the world, even if it was as abstract as pixels and binary code.

It was four in the morning when he finally managed to make the phone admit he existed. It was just one digit but it took. And then Eithe started to fidget feverishly. He ignored her at first, intent on repeating his success. Around them, the sweaty travellers belched and dribbled in their sleep. He hammered at the interior of the screen, which locked itself.

Eithe moaned, and he gave up.

He hissed, 'Eithe. Eithe. Wake up.'

She rolled over and sucked in a nose full of pillow. A frisson passed through her, she rolled over, sat bolt upright and hit her head on the bed above.

'Urgh,' she said.

'Are you okay?'

'Nightmares.'

'Were you dreaming about him?' said the Mirror Man. He meant the German.

'Yes,' said Eithe. She thought he meant Joe.

'Well do something about it,' said the Mirror Man.

'I don't know if I can,' she said. 'It's someone else. Someone else's life. I'm interfering.'

'You have to interfere sometimes,' said the Mirror Man irritably. 'Interfering is part of being alive. Every breath you take interferes with the air. It's either that or be dead.'

'I know that,' said Eithe. She was not happy with what he was saying or the snappish way he said it.

She woke late and the German was at the hatch again. His head was down and he was working through an accounts book. The end of his pen wobbled back and forth as he wrestled with the calculations.

'Doesn't anyone else work here?' The Mirror Man muttered, from the side of the brass bell, in a voice like ringing metal.

Eithe put her hand on it to still the vibrations. 'Morning,' she said to the receptionist.

'*Gut morgen*,' he said, looking up. The Mirror Man scowled. Eithe looked at the receptionist. He was tanned

EITHE'S WAY

and broad-faced, with white teeth. The Mirror Man cleared his throat.

'This is a bit unusual,' said Eithe. 'And I don't know if you can, because of privacy laws and everything, but would it be possible to find someone on the system? They would have stayed here –' she paused as though she was waiting for the next thought. In the brass bell, the Mirror Man signalled with his fingers. 'Oh, about fifteen years ago,' Eithe finished.

The German shook his head. 'It would take some time. We have the written records, before they were transferred to computer. But there are many.'

'I knew it was stupid,' said Eithe. Then there was another pause before she said, 'I don't even know the name. It's not like I could have read them all out anyway, just to see if they sounded familiar.'

The receptionist nodded helpfully.

'Am I interrupting?' said Eithe.

'I like that you interrupt,' he said. 'It means I do not have to do the sums.'

'Oh,' said Eithe. She leaned over the sill and ran an expert eye across the columns. Even upside down, she read the numbers fluently.

'Do you want me to have a look?' The German half-grinned and pushed the book over. To her own utter surprise, she plucked the pen from his hand. 'See, that's wrong,' she said, pointing at an unbalanced multiplication, 'and someone forgot the remainder there. I'm not surprised you're struggling.'

'I speak a lot of languages, but not the language of numbers,' said the German. 'It makes my brain a mess.'

Eithe licked her finger and parted the pages, circling and underlining. The Mirror Man mouthed, 'What are you doing?' at her as she looked up at the German.

'This needs sorting,' she said, and, for the first time, she sounded certain. 'The sooner the better. The longer you leave it, the more it will cost.'

'I see.'

'Why don't you do it on the computer? It's easier to use a spreadsheet. I could set one up that would practically do the work for you.'

The receptionist laughed. 'That would be good.' Eithe offered the German the pen, and he reached just a little too far and closed his fingers around her hand very gently and for a little bit too long. '*Danke*,' he said. 'My name is Gerhardt.'

Eithe was shell-shocked, but the Mirror Man looked unimpressed.

'Sleaze,' he whispered from the barrel of the pen, in a voice like a nib scratching on paper.

'Sorry?'

'Please,' said Eithe. 'Could you tell me where the *Residenz* is? It sounds like it could make for an interesting afternoon.'

He said, 'You wake late. I think perhaps you will not have time there. But, hmmm, I think if you make the right choice, you could have a very interesting evening instead.'

Stars of pale skin spread out from the sides of his eyes, marking his smile lines. Eithe giggled. If his throat hadn't been hundreds of miles away, The Mirror Man might have retched.

'I will see you later,' said the German.

'Okay.' Eithe walked away, but she looked over her shoulder twice before she left.

'You have a crush,' said the Mirror Man, his voice coming through the ring like a coin rolling on a table top. He sounded mildly contemptuous.

'Shut up,' said Eithe.

'Go to the *Residenz* now,' said the Mirror Man. 'Don't wait around for Mr Smooth to take you. Did you see his back when he leant over? He has a tramp stamp.'

'My eyes don't move around as much as yours,' said Eithe, pointedly. She went out into the sunlight and shaded the screen of her phone as walked.

'You're going the wrong way,' said the Mirror Man. 'What are you doing?'

'Just learning how to use it.'

'You don't really need to do that,' he said, but she carried on clicking icons and exploring. 'Please can we move on,' he said wearily. 'There isn't anything for us here. God, I want a cigarette.'

'Maybe we should look for clues in town,' she said.

But his recall of the area was shaky, and her map-reading was poor, and the phone kept loading the wrong page, so it was a while before they found the town centre, and late enough that the market in the square was folding up for the day. Eithe walked among the stalls, deconstructed into crates bristling with asparagus tips or ice impregnated with the smell of fish and then out of the square.

'The Fortress.' The Mirror Man pointed.

The Festung Marienberg loomed over the town, pale grey under a battlement-bitten sky, old and impressive. From somewhere in the town, Eithe could hear a gang of teenage football fans chanting, '*Du, du hast mich…*' with a lusty cheerfulness quite at odds with the meaning of the lyrics.

The Mirror Man seemed uncharacteristically thoughtful as Eithe trekked back through town.

'Eithe!' said Gerhardt, as she came through the door. 'I struggle still. Will you teach me?'

'Yes,' she said. She entered the reception area, switched the computer on, opened up a spreadsheet and started putting commands in place. The German wheeled his chair close, so their legs touched, and she patiently showed him her workings, but he was not a good student, because he kept stealing glances at her instead of looking at the computer screen. She was rapt, and even when he brought out a biscuit and pressed it to her lips, saying 'Here, you need food for the brain,' she didn't respond, pulled into a finite, definite world, oblivious to his flirting.

'You are so naïve,' said the Mirror Man, but she didn't hear him, or the touch of relief in his tone. She worked doggedly at the accounting, unaware of either man. By the evening, Gerhardt was prone on the lower bunk, breathing into the mattress, napping before his night shift. The Mirror Man was stony with frustration, glaring at her from the computer screen, and she was still working, searching through the older books with studious attention. On the television, tiny men kicked a ball around.

'He likes you,' said the Mirror Man, his voice the sound of a clapper ringing lazily in the brass bell.

'I don't know,' said Eithe.

'Oh, he does,' he said. 'He asked you into the office because he wanted a kiss.'

'Leave me alone,' Eithe looked from the page to the screen and added some numbers.

'You can hear him breathing,' said the Mirror Man tightly, as though he was picking at a scab. Eithe twiddled the pencil. In the bunk bed behind her, Gerhardt dozed.

She was aware of his chest expanding and contracting beneath the thin sheet. It was muscular and she wondered whether it was smooth or furred.

The old ledger was a knotted mess of names and numbers. Normally she enjoyed the satisfaction of sorting, but she couldn't concentrate. She heard his skin whisper as he moved under the linen and she shivered.

'Why don't you just fuck him then?' said the Mirror Man, angrily. 'Just do it. Go and fuck him. And then we can get on with it and go.'

Eithe stood up.

The grey lino was dead against the soles of her feet. Gerhardt was still slumped, his head twisted to the side, one arm dangling to the floor, his eyes closed. Blue light flickered across his face. Eithe switched the hissing television off.

Gerhardt muttered, '*Ich hörte auf den.*'

She drew the curtain, draped the blanket from the top bunk across the television and computer, put the brass bell outside and shut the hatch. It trilled angrily. She hoped the Mirror Man would not be able to see, but the window was open and a cold wind blew through, rolling the curtains up so the moon shone through, silvering the pane.

Wafts of cotton lifted in the breeze, exposing the glass as she lifted her hands to her neck and unbuttoned her shirt and trousers until she stood in a puddle of her own clothes. Her form was long and undulant, and there were tufts of soft hair at the junction between her legs and where her arms met her trunk.

She stepped lightly over to the bed. The line of Gerhardt's body was shadowed against the wall, sharp as a knife cut. His cheekbones were shapely, the dimples shallow with relaxation. Eithe breathed and stood and looked, her insides turning to fluid. Slowly, slowly, she stretched out a hand and rested it in the curve between his neck and shoulder. His eyes opened. They were a vivid blue.

She drew the sheet aside and then she settled onto the mattress. His arms curled her close. Wordless, they met lip-to-lip. And then he breathed out and she breathed in and the sweetness of him flooded her lungs. She pressed close so that her breasts squashed against his chest and his fingers sat in the gaps between her ribs as she wriggled her legs apart and made a tiny animal noise. His hands cupped her face and he slid inside her, and they fused together. They started to move, oblivious to the silent watcher.

After a few, long, liquid moments, the Mirror Man turned away, his face a picture of pain.

13

Pulling the File

MR ERWIN LEANED OVER THE well-padded shoulder of Detective Inspector Keane and squinted at the screen. A grainy image showed a tall woman wave her hand at a man standing dead still in the middle of a crowded corridor.

'Eithe Dord,'said Keane. She liked monosyllables. 'She's twenty-six. Lived in Manchester eight years.'

'That sounds like a made up name.'

'It is. They both are,' said Keane.

'Change of ID?' Erwin said. Something about his companion called for clipped, rapid-fire questions and responses. Unlike her body, there was nothing soft about her demeanour.

'Not unless she was on the run from five hours old. The surname her father adopted when he took citizenship. It isn't a real name. I thought he made it up, but when I looked it up, it turned out to be a lexical error in the Webster Dictionary. A word with no provenance. He must have picked it deliberately. And the first name is just rubbish. Some trendy thing like calling your kid Paris or Peaches. A non-name for a non-person.'

'What's her background?'

'She works in accounting for an underwriting firm.'

'Does she have any dodgy connections?'

Keane shrugged. 'Not that we know of. She wasn't a high-up. Just a pen-pusher. Quiet, never got promoted, never got fired. Same job since graduation.' She reached over and restarted the CCTV video. They watched in silence as the tall woman ran into the man, spoke briefly, left him, turned back as he collapsed, took a step toward him, then a step back and finally hurried away.

'Did he pass anything over when they made contact?'

'Could have,' said Keane. 'If they both went to school with Penn and Teller. It would've had to be a very quick exchange. We've got a good angle on them here, and you can see her hands most of the time.'

Erwin sat back in the swivel chair and chewed the inside of his mouth. He was new to the Special Fraud Office, and this was the first time he'd worked with a policeman. He'd assumed Keane would be bringing a box of doughnuts to the meeting, but she hadn't, and he was getting hungry.

'Clean record, although her boyfriend has previous for disturbing the peace and public nuisance. He's a bit of a hippy. Anyway, he's gone AWOL too. Probably sitting in a tent eating lentils in a democracy village or something.

She's utterly boring. She's not so much as sneezed at the wrong time, hasn't made any big purchases, like, ever, no family, nothing. It's like she's not even real.'

'Oh yes?' said Erwin, intrigued. 'Maybe it's a deep cover.'

'If it is, it's crap. Fake identities have substance, otherwise they don't work. Anyway, this is what we have: there's this ten second romance. We swept the flat, found prints on the table. They matched ones we took from her desk at the office. She paid him a personal visit. That's it so far.'

'It'll take a while to go through the papers,' said Erwin. 'At the moment we're not sure there's anything in his private concerns that implicate him. We've found an account in the Caymans, but there's nothing illegal about it, even if it's unethical.'

'We're in the shit a bit,' said Keane. 'It'll be difficult to trace her. As long as she stays in the Schengen zone, she'll just flash her passport and walk through the boundaries.'

'But he's all we've got.'

'And she's all we've got on him. So she'll have to do.'

'We'll have to get Interpol on this.'

'No,' said Keane, at once. 'This is our jurisdiction.'

'Do you fancy a snack?' Erwin said hopefully. 'I could run to the tuck shop.'

'Nah, I'm on the Red and Green diet,' said Keane.

Flight

THEY WERE STILL A TANGLE when the sun came up. Eithe rose first, and pulled herself loose while Gerhardt stretched on the mattress until his tendons crackled. 'Inge will be here soon, and I will take you to town.'

'Okay,' said Eithe, and she retreated to the bathroom.

'Was it worth it?' The Mirror Man said as she cleansed her skin.

'I don't know.'

'You know you don't need to screw the first man you meet,' he said.

'Why do you care, Mirror Man?' she said, scraping at the thatch of her underarms with a half-blunt razor. 'What's it to you?'

'I don't care,' he said. 'It's nothing.'

'Right.' She ran the razor under the tap and then turned back to the mirror, set her forefinger under one eye and drew it down. 'I wish you'd get out of the way. I need to see what I look like.'

'Why?'

'I want to put some makeup on.'

'That's okay, I'll tell you if you smudge.' She gave him a sceptical look. 'You won't trust me?'

'Should I?'

He sighed. 'I promise I won't make you draw a moustache,' said the Mirror Man, and she risked it, running kohl around her eyes with a tentative hand. She brushed at the up-tilted corner of her eye with the pad of her forefinger, blending. 'You look fine,' said the Mirror Man.

'Really?'

'Yes. Freckles, philtrum and fawn skin,' he said. 'Everything's still there.'

'Fawn? I always thought it was boring beige.'

'What about me?' said the Mirror Man.

'Narcissist,' she said, working on the other eye.

'Am I that beautiful?' he said.

She imagined Narcissus, polished, gilded, his muscles still under shining skin, face duplicated, nose to nose, lip to lip in clear, unpolluted, unmoving water. She looked at the Mirror Man, with his mossy chin and grey visage, and did not know how to lie. 'He was vain,' she said. 'And selfish.'

'I'm not vain.'

'Actually,' said Eithe, and she put down the eye pen, 'you don't look great.'

'Thanks.'

'No, really. You look ill.'

'Describe it,' he said.

'You are very thin,' she said, 'and your skin looks a bit yellow. There's dark around your eyes, and the veins are showing through like little blue worms.'

'You are a poet, Eithe, but stop moving your mouth and put some lipstick on it.'

When she finished, she showed her teeth so he could check them for smears of red. She looked troubled as she put her makeup back in its pouch.

'What?' he said.

'Narcissus drowned,' she said. 'He forgot all about his thirst, food, drink and sleep, and about everything except himself. Someone should have pulled him back, away from the water.'

'Go on, Eithe.'

For an instant, the Mirror Man's control failed and he looked fragile and cold. But Eithe didn't catch the lapse or the smirk he quickly marshalled into place, helped by the smudge of powder left on her temple. She was already turning to leave the room.

Gerhardt wiped the makeup off with his thumb before they set off. 'Why did you come here?' he said, as they walked across the white bridge.

'Oh, just to get away,' she said as the path bottlenecked, cramped with stalls selling painted tiles and bangles.

'Now look there.' He pointed. 'Do you see the vine fields? The Würzburg region yields a golden wine. Tomorrow I will have you try a glass.' The road twisted up the hill. 'There,' he said, 'that is the Residenz.'

'I'd like to visit.'

'It's pretty boring, but sure.'

They walked until they halted by a set of massive gates. The building was cool stone, elegant, high and

many-windowed. Thin threads of music filtered across the
courtyard, plucked notes pattering like falling blossom.
Gerhardt poked her gently on the nose. 'Why do you stop?'

'Because it's beautiful.'

When the passage of the concerto ended, Eithe
bought the tickets and they walked into an empty hall
which stretched out in every direction. Squat white arches
supported the ceiling. At the far end, a staircase rose, split
into two and flowed into the upper floor. The Mirror Man
slid through the marble.

Eithe's lips parted as she looked up.

'Pretty, huh?' said Gerhardt.

'Yes.'

Eithe was lost in clouds, cracks of blue sky and rays
of sunlight, trying to memorise the details, the folds of
cloth, the feathered head-dresses, the faces of the alabaster
statues at each corner, with their biceps flexed to carry the
sky. When she felt so full of colour and light that she could
take no more, they toured the smaller rooms dripping with
gilt and heavy hangings, and looked at the bed Napoleon
once slept in. Some of the walls were still propped up with
scaffolding or covered in tarpaulin.

Gerhardt looked up at the ravaged ceiling.

'What happened here?' said Eithe.

'I don't know, perhaps the damp, with the stuff of the
walls lumping away.'

In the garden, fauns wrestled with putti on a sandstone
balustrade. Eithe and Gerhardt followed the sweep of
the stairs and passed along a shaded arbour. They found a
fountain bordered by flowerbeds stuffed with orange tulips
and brilliant blossoms. Eithe perched by the bubbling
water, and the Mirror Man watched them from each

scintillating splash. Dryads and hamadryads hid in the branches of the encircling evergreens.

Gerhardt settled beside her. 'Mmm,' said Eithe. The sunlight on his skin was making his blood rise. He had a pleasant, savoury scent.

'So what's your story?'

'I have no story,' he said. 'Here I am.' The conversation lapsed. He tapped a finger on her knee. 'You worry a lot,' said Gerhardt.

'Yes,' said Eithe. '*Agito ergo sum.*'

'What do you worry about?'

'Making the right choice,' she said. 'Before it's too late.'

'*Torschkusspanik,*' said Gerhardt.

Eithe looked quizzical.

'You get old, you run out of time, you run out of chances.'

'What do you worry about?' said Eithe.

'I do not wish for my team to be relegated.'

'Oh,' she said.

The flowers nodded their heads. There was a moment of quiet. In the space between their words, the water flowed. He toyed with her hair, pulling it long and letting it spring back into shape. They could have kissed then, but whatever had fizzed between them had stilled.

Spooked Quarry

IN THE EVENING, EITHE STOKED up the antique computer in the kitchen. It made a change from the tiny phone screen.

The Mirror Man sounded digital and crackly from the speakers.

'When I visited, the Residenz was in terrible disrepair,' he said. 'The Allies bombed it during the war and split the roof open. The rain came in and with it, the mould. Things went green. The walls began to fall away. It was quite sad, really. After the bombings, they tried to restore some of the images, but they used chemicals which ate into the walls and blistered the paint, or peeled it off and did more damage than good.'

'See, this is the problem,' said Eithe. 'You never know what's right.'

'They did what they thought was best at the time,' he said. 'And now there are dedicated people still working on the building. Much was saved. The painting on the ceiling is the largest fresco in the world. The women you saw represent the continents, Africa, Asia, America and here. When you travel, you walk across Europe's belly.'

'Why are you telling me this?'

'Because Gerhardt didn't.'

'He is actually quite dull, isn't he?' she laughed. 'But good looking.'

'Is it a bratwurst,' the Mirror Man said, slyly, 'or mini frankfurter?'

'Don't be unpleasant.'

'Will you be rounding off your evening with a bit of German sausage?'

'Shush and let me read my emails,' said Eithe. 'Juliette replied.'

Dear Eithe,

We are well, thank you.

It is always good to hear from friends and guests: they are our family, as our family will not be so. I would say: please come back and stay with us next year, but it may be that the Rainbow will not be open. Our financial troubles are too big. Do not worry about the ring. It is my gift to you. This is the ring my mother gave to me, for a man to put on me when I married him. Perhaps I could pawn it for the hostel, but I wish for you to carry it until you can put it to a use. Your own man came to the hostel just yesterday. If you do not mind me to say, but he is very strange. He says you will meet in Würzburg soon.

Eithe felt her faint smile wither as she read the last line.
Her features petrified into an unmoving configuration.

'What is it?'

'He went to the Rainbow,' she said. 'He went to the
Rainbow and he's coming here.'

She was deathly calm and methodical as she shut the
computer down, went into the dormitory and began to
stuff her clothes and toiletries into the case. She checked
the journal, scanning the ticket pasted on to the dog-eared
page, before she tucked it into her pocket.

'Eithe, where do you go?' said Gerhardt, as she strode
into the reception to recover her coat and passport.

'I have to leave. I'm sorry Gerhardt,' and to the
annoyance of the Mirror Man, she stooped to enter his
embrace and kissed the top of his head as she handed him
the money. 'This should cover the bill.'

'Sure, sure, Eithe, but where do you go?' he
said, mystified.

'Maybe it's better if I don't tell you. Goodbye.'

'Eithe?'

But she was gone.

The Stranger

GERHARDT SAT AT THE HATCH. He faced a long night alone. The door creaked open, and the fluorescent tubes flickered. When they stabilised, they seemed weak and wan, but the shadows were richer, in defiance of the laws of light.

The stranger was tall, but his shoulders were rounded and he slouched with tiredness. He smelled faintly of sweat and he was wrinkled from long travelling. He had no luggage.

Gerhardt, not usually an introvert, was so absorbed in thought that the stranger hammered the little clapper inside its brass shell. Gerhardt looked up. The stranger's eyes burned red-rimmed in a pale, ragged face. They roved, searching the shaded places, and they did not rest.

'Hi.'

'*Guten tag*,' said Gerhardt automatically.

'Shut up,' said Joe to the wall. The receptionist had to stop himself from recoiling. The stranger's breath was foul after five days of unbrushed teeth and black coffee taken on the move.

'Not you, sorry.'

'What's your name?' asked Gerhardt, reaching for the ledger.

'Joe. Joe King.'

Gerhardt began to smile. Joe barked, 'Don't laugh. I'm looking for someone.'

He slid a photograph across the table. Gerhardt wasn't surprised to see Eithe. They sat on a sofa and his arm was slung over her shoulders. It would have been a pleasant picture, except that, instead of resting loosely, Joe's fingers were fastened around her flesh. She was looking at him while he stared at the camera as if to say: see what I have. He had a *backpfeifengesicht*, a face Gerhardt wanted to punch.

'Stop waving your arms,' said the stranger, but he was not talking to the receptionist.

Gerhardt worked hard to control the muscles in his jaw. 'She has not stayed here,' he said, his words clipped and precise.

'Are you sure?' Joe leaned in, his slumping face suddenly tight with tension. 'No one else booked her in? Think hard.'

'We have not enough staff,' said Gerhardt. 'I am here often enough to have met every guest who has stayed here this week. I do not know who she is.'

'Are you sure?' Joe said again. Gerhardt met his eyes. It was not a nice experience. There was something wild and desperate worming in Joe's face. His pupils zipped like mayflies.

'Yes.'

The pale eyes stopped searching the shadows and met Gerhardt's. The air sizzled. There was a nasty moment. Joe glared at him with a cocktail of suspicion and jealousy. Gerhardt did not blink.

'Okay,' Joe said. There was no warmth in the words. When he went away, the room seemed brighter.

'He was lying,' said Gemma, once they were outside. She was muffled by the night. 'Arsehole.'

'It has nothing to do with you,' said Joe.

'I'm sorry,' she said, but her impossible silhouette, split three ways by the street lamp, did not look sorry, with its high chin and firm shoulders. 'I'm just a romantic. Nothing should get in the way of true love.'

'No,' said Joe. 'It shouldn't.'

Flowering

'ARE YOU UPSET?' SAID THE Mirror Man, as she looked dismally out at the view. He was not trying hard to hide his pleasure at leaving.

The carriage travelled along bridges and through the forest which closed thick and dark around the tracks. Wooden chalets with shutters, steep roofs and peeking windows grew from the ground. Then the mountains rose up, high and craggy.

'There are people around,' she reminded him.

'Seriously,' he said. 'You can't be sad.'

'Well I am.'

'You weren't infatuated with him,' he said.

'No, but he was sweet, and he didn't understand.'

'Like a big stupid dog,' he said.

'Perhaps.'

'Did he like being hit with a rolled up magazine?'

She cast a quick glance, but the carriage was almost deserted, with only a kid curled up under a coat, trainers sticking out, and an elderly woman with her head flopping forward. 'As if you don't know,' she said in an undertone.

'I don't,' he said.

'So you weren't watching all the time.'

'No, I wasn't' he said. 'But you thought I was, and you did it anyway. Not such a good girl after all. Did you fuck him just because I told you to? That really would be sad, unless it was because of the contract. Bloody hell, I could have done with a PA like you. Hey, Eithe. Rub your stomach and pat your head at the same time.' When she didn't move, he continued, 'Tell me, was all that stuff with the books some kind of mathematical seduction technique?'

'I was going through the books to find you,' she said. 'I finished the spreadsheet in a few hours. The rest of the time I was cross-referencing dates and arrivals to see if I could find your name.'

'Oh,' he said, somewhat taken aback. 'You tricked him.' He sounded impressed. 'You know, I think that underneath your woolly-ness, I think there's actually a functioning mind.'

'It didn't work anyway.'

She wiped her nose and turned away from his face, speckled in the dirt-spattered window. She sucked in her cheeks, put her head back against the rest and closed her eyes. She feigned sleep for a moment, but then she said, 'I didn't do it to prove a point, or to get back at Joe, or even because you told me to do it. I wanted to feel it.'

'What?'

'It. What Juliette called *jouissance*.'

'Oh,' he said. 'An orgasm.'

Her eyes whipped open.

'Shhh.'

'We're on the continent. People are as likely to know what you mean by *jouissance* as orgasm.'

'Shush!' she said, scandalised, but on the edge of laughter.

The first rays of the sun were dyed by the filth on the window. The jerk of the brakes made ripples run through his surface. 'So never,' he said, 'have you ever had one?'

'No.'

'How long were you with Joe? You had him for years, and you didn't show him how to make you come?'

Eithe winced. 'It's difficult to teach someone something you don't know how to do yourself. Now I'm going to sleep.' She shut her eyes again and ersatz snores filtered across the space between them.

'Eithe?' he said. 'Keep on talking.'

'Why?' she said, muffled by her collar.

'I want to be distracted.'

But she was sinking and her breathing evolved into real snores.

When the train pulled into the next station, the sign read: *Bad Gastein*.

The exit led to a tube of white struts and corrugated metal that stretched above the main road. Her first dizzied view of the town was of cars speeding under her feet. The streak of asphalt was a pale tongue licking at the edge of dawn.

The town clumped along the left side of the road. On the right, the ground swelled and rolled and humped up until it disappeared into a bank of cloud. Mizzle settled on her hair as she entered the hotel.

Her single room was small, simple and clean. She stowed her bag under the bed, stripped off and showered. Her skin tingled under the stream of water. She didn't care about the eyes in the mirror. When she was dressed, she switched the light off, pushed past the curtain and stepped out onto the balcony.

A fingernail sliver hovered silver on the horizon, the moon's last wink before it set. The town was sketched in fine lines, light marking the straight edges of roofs, walls and kerbs. The mountain lurked as though it was waiting to smash down like a black wave. On the other side of the road, streetlamps shone in hard white haloes.

Eithe was twitchy. She sat at the dressing table and emailed Juliette.

I'm sorry to hear about your money troubles. If you want, I can look through your books. It will save you the cost of an accountant.

I am in Bad Gastein now.

Keep in touch,

Eithe.

She fidgeted. 'Go to sleep,' said the Mirror Man. 'Whatever it is that's here, you have to find it tomorrow. You'll need your energy.'

Then a spasm of pain passed through him.

'What was that?' she said.

'I don't know. Something's happening.'

'What?' said Eithe.

He shook with another seismic shudder, and his sallow skin blanched. There was an impact which shook his distant organs like balloons in a breeze. His lips were tight and his teeth barely parted as he sighed. A wash of lassitude came over him.

'Hey,' said Eithe. She rapped on the glass. 'Come back.' His eyes were rolling into the back of his head. 'Hey,' she pressed her palm to the cold surface. 'Pull back. Come on.'

'Ugh,' he said.

'Don't you drift away,' she said. 'Don't you dare go and leave me here on my own.'

'I'm here,' he said. 'I'm here, I'm here.'

Eithe sat back in the scroll-armed chair. She was breathing hard. 'Okay,' she said. 'Okay, okay.' They gazed at each other. 'How do you feel?'

'Hollow. Something is slowly failing. My vacant tissue. It's not just the nothing. I'm still too close to home. Got to go further.'

'You aren't making sense.'

'I'm all right.'

She could see the effort it cost him to draw his attention to her and reassemble his consciousness. 'I'll hurry,' she said. 'I'll ask the receptionist about the records.'

'No,' he said. 'It doesn't hurt anymore. You seem tired. Go and rest.'

She looked as though she was on the verge of argument, but then she nodded and took herself to bed.

In the morning she woke with a jolt and looked straight at the mirror.

'It's time to leave,' he said.

'No,' she said. 'I'm going to try to find your identity. Whatever it is.'

She threw back the eiderdown and grabbed her clothes, dressed and marched downstairs.

'Hi,' she said to the receptionist. 'I'm trying to find out if a specific person stayed here about ten years ago. Can I have a look at the records?'

But the receptionist, a young woman, valued her job and knew about privacy law and data protection, and she refused. No amount of persuasion could budge her, and when the Mirror Man, whispering through a silver ballpoint pen, suggested a bribe, Eithe gave up in disgust and returned to her room.

'I'm not doing that,' she said, and to her surprise, the Mirror Man agreed.

'I think we should stop looking through hostel records,' he said. 'They won't go back that far and even if they do, no one else would be stupid enough to let you search through them.'

Instead, Eithe re-checked the journal, smoothed out the time-yellowed ticket and peered at the details. It was for the Felsentherme mountain spa.

She hadn't thought to pack swimwear during her mad dash from the house, but they let her in anyway and gave her a robe which she put over her bare skin. She prowled past steamed glass and pools full of screaming, splashing children hurling themselves from diving boards. The floor was blood temperature and the air was humid. She reached the top level. As she walked through the upper complex of hot tubs and cold pools, an attendant came up and tweaked her sleeve.

'No robe,' he said.

Eithe retreated to a changing room to remove the garment.

'Brave,' said the Mirror Man. He didn't sound sarcastic.

'Well, we have to check everywhere.'

She walked, awkward as a wading bird, past a woman vigorously towelling her buttocks and a chubby man whose smug belly bulged above two little hazelnuts and a cashew.

The last set of stairs led to the outside world. Eithe gasped as the mountain air hit her clammy flesh and chilled her until she puckered. She forgot her shame and bolted for the outdoor pool and wallowed into the water. At once, the geothermal heat penetrated her flesh and she breathed more easily. The liquid covered her like a slick blanket.

The Mirror Man's reflection fluctuated in the water. His face looked as though it was wrapped in plastic. 'Nothing,' he said. 'There's nothing here. No reminders.'

Eithe had nothing to say. She looked across the mountainside, over the saw-tooth jag of the trees, into the far distance. 'How are you feeling?' she asked, eventually.

'Desperate.'

'So am I,' she said, into the foam. 'So am I.' She lay back against the side, lifted her legs and let herself float. Her toes rose out of the water. 'Beige,' she said, with disgust.

'Who told you that?'

'Joe.'

'He was right,' said the Mirror Man.

'You are a dickhead.'

'Do you know the colour of the light of the universe?'

'No'

'The astronomers thought it was mint green,' said the Mirror Man. 'But it isn't. They miscalibrated their instruments. It's beige.'

'Mmm.'

Eithe stretched sumptuously.

'Maybe Gerhardt did you good,' the Mirror Man said, his voice coming grudgingly from the misted tiles. She sloshed the lukewarm water gently with her twirling fingers.

'Why's that?'

'You're not so prudish now. You are unwinding.'

'Oh,' she said. 'No. I suppose you don't really count.' He didn't reply, but for an instant the hurt was visible on his face. Her words smote him. 'Back home, the narcissi will be out by now,' said Eithe, mollifying. 'Why did you stare into the mirror? Was it because you were handsome?'

'I don't really want to talk about it.'

'Tell me,' she said.

'Don't make fun of me,' he said.

'I won't.'

'For as long I saw myself I felt—' He stopped. She tapped the tile to prompt him. 'Real,' he blurted. Eithe saw the skin under his stubble flood with pink. 'As though I had worth. I used to have value.'

'You still seem to have a high opinion of yourself.'

'Not arrogance,' he said, and for the first time he seemed if not ashamed, then at least self-conscious. 'Value is different to vanity.'

'Ah.'

He grimaced with embarrassment. 'I suppose it was something I couldn't find in other people.'

Eithe laughed. She couldn't help it. 'I understand,' she said. 'I'm lonely too.'

The Mirror Man let himself lap against her.

'Eithe,' he said. 'You don't have a mark on you.' She looked startled, and he pulled away. 'I should have drowned that before it came out,' he said. 'It's a weird thing to say. I don't know why I said it.'

Eithe stopped his almost-apology dead when she said, 'He never broke the skin.' The mist rolled down the mountain. The air went grey. The sun sank, its circumference frilled by the mountain ridge. Eithe's breathing generated little rings in the water, the edges tipped with borrowed light. She could feel the mist coruscating at the back of her throat.

'Oh, Eithe. I didn't mean that,' the Mirror Man foundered. 'I meant – you've got good skin. No – that sounds racist. I mean it's smooth-'

Eithe took pity on him.

'My feet are getting calloused,' she said. 'Especially after today.'

'If I could, I'd rub them,' he said.

She kicked at the surface until it lathered, and he laughed from the iridescence of a thousand bubbles.

Eavesdropping

JOE SAT IN THE SOULLESS bar of the businessman's stopover. Rage made him dampen the sporadic conversations his coma-stricken companion tried to spark up.

The girl at the bar was stupid. He found himself speaking loud and slow, stabbing his finger on the menu and miming the twist and crick of a ring-pull. The money he handed over was Monopoly cash. He swallowed the ball of burning fury in his throat and told himself it was fate and that he and Eithe would meet further down the line.

He would never give up. Joe was no linguist, so he didn't know the German word *liebestod*, but it was a perfect fit for his fantasies. He wanted to keep Eithe and love her for the rest of his life, and hers, and if that was only possible by killing them both, then that was what he would do. He checked his phone again, again and again. What if she flew home? He wanted to be sure he was still on her trail, so he phoned the police back in England.

'I want to report a missing person,' he said, when they picked up. 'It's my fiancée, her surname is Dord. She vanished six days ago. I think she was drunk. She doesn't drink. I phoned her work and they said she hasn't been in. It's not like her. She's very methodical, very set in her ways. She keeps a strict routine. She's a bit, you know, vulnerable. She has mental problems.

'At first I just thought she was stressed about the wedding and had gone away to think, but I read about the woman, the one who was attacked in her flat. I'm really worried something has happened to her. Last I heard, she was in Germany, but she might come back to the UK any time.'

The woman on the end of the line was sympathetic and took down the details. As he closed the call, the waitress put a plate down in front of him. He eyed the mess in an orange sauce. His teeth bounced off the tough flesh as he chewed. It could have been offal, connective tissue, the gristly end of a bone or a bottom feeder from around a volcanic vent.

Gemma was still talking when he went to bed. He lay down and, with the shadow so close to his ear, it was hard to ignore her. 'And anyway, why did you learn sign language?' she said.

'I volunteered at a centre for people with disabilities,' he said. 'Before I went to university.'

'That's nice,' she said.

'I wish more people thought that,' he said. 'Some people told me it was pointless.'

'They're just jealous,' said Gemma. 'They don't have the motivation or imagination. You shouldn't be so sensitive.'

'People laugh at me,' he said. 'They always have.'

'I don't think you're funny,' she said.

'Even my family laughed at me,' he said. 'Or at least, he laughed and they did nothing to stop him.'

'Who?'

'Mr King, when I was little. He took my books and threw them away.'

'There was nothing you could have done,' said Gemma, who was not given to pointless retrospection.

'I know.'

'Come here,' said Gemma, moved by his little-boy distress, and she wrapped him in a shadowy hug.

Joe tolerated the spectral touch for a few moments and then pulled free.

He hesitated over the light switch. If he kept it on, he was afraid Gemma would sweep her arms around him again and babble her horribly cheerful chatter right into his ear. But if he turned the light off, his whole world would be steeped in shadow, and he might never escape. It reminded him of his childhood agonies, when he lay with a full bladder, too afraid to go to the toilet because of an imagined hand coming out from under the bed to grasp his ankle.

'Is something wrong?' she said.

'Where have you been, the last few nights?' he said. 'Have you been in the dark behind the door, or inside the wardrobe, or down the plughole?'

'No,' she said. 'I'm not anywhere. I can't see, but I know when it's morning, because the world comes back. You come back. Will you leave the light on for me?'

'No,' he said and switched the light off.

She weltered in the black.

In the morning, at a dry, bread-heavy breakfast, he checked the phone again. Gemma was softly sobbing, stretched across the tired carpet.

The fork dropped as he bolted for the door, leaving the meal uneaten. He hauled the shadow with him.

Helping
with Enquiries

AT DAWN THE NEXT DAY, Eithe was woken by the
ringing telephone. Dazed, she reached for the smartphone,
but it didn't matter how many times she swiped the screen,
the sound kept coming. Eventually she lifted the old
Bakelite receiver, dropped it, retrieved it and then said,
'Yes?'

'*Fräulein*? Hallo?' said the receptionist. 'There are some
people here to see you.'

She said, 'Okay,' but she didn't put the phone down.

'People,' said the Mirror Man. 'Not a person. Maybe
not him. Ask what they look like.'

'What are they like?' she croaked.

'A woman and an older gentleman.'

'Okay.' She pulled her clothes on over her pyjamas and went downstairs without brushing her teeth. Her fingers snagged in her hair as she entered the reception area, and she had to pull them free.

'Miss Jones,' said the woman, with a sceptical lift of an eyebrow.

Some flash of self-preservation stopped Eithe from saying 'Who?' Instead, she went, 'Okay.'

'I'm Detective Inspector Keane.'

'And I'm from the Serious Fraud Office,' said Erwin. 'I'm not with the police. I'm an investigator. I do what you do, sort of, but in reverse. It's numerical forensics.'

'We would like to have a little chat with you,' said Keane, cutting in before her colleague embarrassed himself. She flipped her ID wallet open and shut.

'Oh shit,' said the Mirror Man, from the whites of the policewoman's eyes.

'Please come with us.'

There was a driver waiting outside. Eithe hesitated at the car door. Maybe Detective Inspector Keane would press her head down as she entered. Perhaps there weren't any handles on the inside. But instead, the policewoman just sat in the front passenger seat and waited.

'Get in the car,' said the Mirror Man from the window. 'You can't run for it. Just – when they interview you, hold the ring to your ear and listen to me.'

'Okay,' said Eithe. The SFO accountant didn't seem to notice, but Keane shot her a sharp look.

It was a normal car. Eithe could have slipped the seatbelt, opened the door and rolled out if she'd needed to, but she wouldn't have known the first thing about running from the law. 'My train is in two hours,' she said. Keane showed no sign of having heard, but Erwin gave her a sympathetic smile as the car rolled forward.

They took her to the small police station, and signed her in as Miss Jones at the front desk. The interview room was sparse. There was no two-way mirror. There was only a table, a telephone and three chairs. Keane indicated the lone chair. Eithe sat down, and Erwin settled on the opposite side of the table. But Keane stood and, for a few seconds, she simply stared at Eithe, appraising her. A girl, she thought, with big eyes and fear in her. But it could be an act.

'You aren't Miss Casey Jones,' she said.

'Admit it,' said the Mirror Man.

'No,' said Eithe. 'I'm Eithe.'

'Dord.'

'Yes.'

'So why do you have a card saying Jones?'

'Ask them if this is an official interview. Ask them if you are under arrest,' said the Mirror Man.

'Am I under arrest?' said Eithe.

'No,' said Keane. The unspoken 'not yet' was buried in the pause she left before adding, 'You are just helping us out.'

'Ask how you can do that.'

'How can I help you?' Eithe said, politely. Under the table, she rubbed the knuckles of her free hand against the wood until they hurt.

'You can tell us the truth.'

She didn't wait for the Mirror Man to tell her what to say.

'Whatever he said I did, I didn't,' she blurted. 'He just wants me to come home, that's all. And I – I'm not sure I want to. I'm not a missing person. Not exactly. I mean, you can't make me go back just because he wants me to.'

'Who's "he"?' said Erwin.

'Joe,' said Eithe. She looked perplexed. 'Isn't that why you're here?'

'The fiancé,' said Keane. 'No. He's not why we're here. We're here about a friend of yours. You're using his card. A conveniently common surname, an ambiguous given name. Could be a man, could be a woman.'

'He gave me the PIN,' said Eithe. 'I didn't steal it.' She heard the Mirror Man groan.

'Miss Dord,' said Erwin, gently. 'We're not accusing you of anything. We have footage of you talking to a man in a railway station. We have what we believe are your prints at a key location – and we will confirm that shortly. If necessary we could do a DNA test, but we're pretty sure we can pin you to the place.'

'Is he in trouble?' asked Eithe.

'Not exactly,' said Erwin, choosing his words carefully. 'At the moment we're just trying to draw on some leads. We know his flat was purchased by the company, and he leases it for a peppercorn rent, like a few of his colleagues. We know he works for the company. But things are a little muddled right now. We suspect that a number of instances of high level fraud have been carried out at the company, and one of the managers, who has disappeared, by the way, shredded a lot of the documents, including employee files. A number of people have gone missing. We checked all of the company-owned flats. Your prints were found in one, but all the records as to whoever was renting it from the company have been destroyed. We are presuming it belongs to whoever is bankrolling you through that account. And that person is the man you were talking to at the station.'

'Eithe,' said the Mirror Man, a quiet but emphatic warning in her ear. She nodded.

'He may not be implicated in the fraud, but we believe he will have information somewhere that could lead us in the right direction.

'You might be wondering why we haven't just interviewed him,' said Keane.

Eithe did not know how to respond.

'He is currently – indisposed,' said Erwin.

'He's dying,' said the policewoman, flatly.

'What is his name?' said Erwin.

'I don't know,' said Eithe. Her ears began shrill with a constant, piercing noise, like the sine tone from the TV test card that had scared her at 3am when she was a child. The paste diamond stayed silent.

'We need to know,' said Erwin. 'Somebody went through his personal documents and destroyed every one of them – insurance, car information, bank details, everything with his name on. The doctors can't access his medical records, as they don't have his details, so there's no way of knowing if there is a degenerative condition contributing to the organ failure.'

'Organ failure,' said Eithe. Her voice was dull. She felt as though the room was filling up with water.

'So you see,' said Keane, from very, very far away. 'It's not just the investigation. It's him as well. If you have any information, any at all, you have to share it.'

'Ask them if they have a warrant to keep you here,' said the Mirror Man. He sounded bruised. 'Ask them if you can leave.'

'I don't know his name,' said Eithe. 'He's just someone I bumped into. He asked me to go to his flat to do him a favour. So I did. But I couldn't help him. I just couldn't. I can't.'

'That's it?' said Keane.

'I'm sorry. Do I have to stay here?'

The policewoman stood, the chair grinding against the floor.

'I will give you our details,' she said. Every part of her, the drawn muscles in her neck, the control of her words, spoke of deep frustration. 'If anything occurs to you, anything at all, let us know straight away, whatever time it is.'

'Shake their hands,' said the Mirror Man, and Eithe obeyed automatically.

There was no suggestion of a lift back to the hostel and the bus was late. By the time Eithe cleared her room, she had missed the train back to Munich. She paced back and forth through the lobby as she waited, unaware of the receptionist trying not to stare too openly at her, until the Mirror Man lost his temper and shouted, 'For God's sake, just go for a walk.'

Brief

ERWIN WAS FILLING IN THE paperwork when his colleague cleared her throat.

'We will have to keep an eye on her,' said Keane. 'She might have more to do with this than she thinks.'

'You're not going to freeze the account.'

'No,' said Keane. 'We can use her transactions to trace her. Christ knows how many other little troves he has hidden away. We don't want them tapping an untracked account. This way we'll have her on a long leash.'

This Americanism sounded right to Erwin. It almost made up for the lack of doughnuts.

Men in the Mist

EITHE FOLLOWED THE STRUTS OF the cable car over ground spongy with recent rain. It was early in the year but the snow had left the lower slopes. Little snaking tracks had been worn in the russet dirt, and her feet found them naturally. Unseasonal alpine flowers grazed her legs as she walked, and the dew soaked the ankles of her jeans. Maybe Joe was right about climate chaos, she thought, in a disconnected way. She walked through dew and mud, slipping on the slick scrub and scrambling over rocks and tussocks. The cable cut a straight black line across the white firmament. The trees closed, flanking the skyway. Eithe found herself picking between stumps and felled logs. When she looked up, she gazed into cloud. The air she sucked in was wet. The crunch of her footsteps on pine needles sounded very far away. She couldn't hear birdcall or any animal sounds. She was walking in nothing.

The cable, half way between the supporting struts, sagged low to the ground. A cabin clanked overhead.

'I'm going to ride the mist,' said the Mirror Man.

Eithe walked on in silence, and he followed her in the millions of microscopic droplets floating in the air. He looked almost real. Sometimes other shapes in the mist looked like people. The rocks became hunched backs and the wind-battered saplings became standing figures with skeleton arms.

'Do you remember where you work?' she asked.

'No,' he said.

'What was the company?'

'I don't know.'

'You do.'

'No.'

'Tell me.'

'It was a bank,' he said. 'A big bank.' And when he told her the name of the bank, she was not surprised.

'Did you take part in the fraud?'

'Alleged fraud,' he said.

'I suppose you just can't remember,' she said bitterly.

The Mirror Man scrambled for an excuse, and when one didn't come, he attacked instead.

'*NO!*' he said, a million massed molecules speaking in unison. His voice reverberated like localised thunder.

Eithe did not quail. 'You can't hit me,' she said, unperturbed. 'I'm not afraid of you. But I think you are afraid of something. Please tell me what it is.' Her quiet, dignified words hobbled his anger.

'They were right. It's killing me. Human beings aren't meant to live asunder.' The mist swirled. 'And what then?' he said, as quiet as rolling tears. 'Ask me what's the worst thing about it all.'

'Tell me,' she whispered.

'There is nothing I can do about it on my own. Nothing at all. That it is down to you. It is your choice. I have never relied on anybody, ever. And now I am powerless.'

His words were a torrent of rage, but she stood, her lips taut and her face stricken, and they subsided. 'I'm going to the hostel,' said Eithe. 'I'm going to get my stuff. Then I'm going to the station.'

She staggered, her mind pressed flat with panic. Disorientated and white-blinded, she fumbled on for what felt like a century. The ground was soft with mulch, but pitted with pine cones and pebbles. The Mirror Man billowed out behind her like a cloak. Then there was a flicker in the fog.

There was a man in the trees.

He was staring at them with such a terrible intensity that there could be no doubt who he was. He peeled out of the branches like a ghoul, murder on his mind. He moved easily – the fog blurred his shadow so it barely dragged his feet.

'Eithe, he's here,' said the Mirror Man. 'To the right.'

Eithe's head whipped round and saw the silhouette, grey against white.

She started to run.

Eithe was not a natural athlete. She did not move with grace. Her lanky legs were loose with dread and she blundered down the slope, sliding on the slippery grass. Joe, despite his lean form, was strong and fuelled by fury, and he was closing the ground between them. She wasn't breathing properly, sobbing with fear, her lungs starved of oxygen.

She keeled over, chest heaving.

'Carry on,' said the Mirror Man. 'Keep going. He's coming after us.'

'Can't,' she said, between gasps.

'You have to,' he said.

She forced herself up, ribs red and screaming with stitch, and ran.

'One, two, three, four,' she panted, and she found her rhythm. 'One, two, three, four,' and slowly, slowly, she drew away. Joe carved a tunnel through the water droplets, his hair flying, his face fixed.

'There's a cable car station just down there,' said the Mirror Man.

'No,' Eithe rasped. 'No time.'

'If you don't, he will.'

So she jinked and dodged as Joe receded into the bank of cloud, still there, still chasing. She turned an abrupt left and hammered into the yawning mouth of the station. She paused at the booth, her knees quivering, her fingers fumbling as she counted the coins.

'Don't buy a fucking ticket!' screamed the Mirror Man. 'Just jump the gate!'

Eithe ignored him. 'All the way down,' she said to the girl at the desk, who printed off the pass with infuriating slowness. Eithe glanced over her shoulder and took the ticket as the girl posted it through the turntable.

The machine slurped it into the slot and spat the ticket back out. Eithe grabbed it and rammed at the turnstile, which jammed and then, mercifully, cycled her through. She jumped into the first cab and the door ground shut, just as Joe slid past the ticket booth like an oiled fish and leaped the gate.

The car swung into the air.

She crouched against the plastic seat, her back to the decline. The car juddered as it passed one of the cable supports, but Eithe didn't even notice.

Joe's face appeared at the window of the following car. He watched her every second of the descent, but Eithe ignored the prickles on the back of her neck and held the Mirror Man's gaze. Her chest heaved.

The cable lowered her into the bottom station and Eithe scrabbled at the door, bolting out of the box. She heard raised voices behind her as she fled, and risked a backward glance.

A ticket attendant had his hand on Joe's chest, and Joe was gesticulating furiously.

She put her head down and sprinted helter-skelter to the railway station. There were two trains, one at each platform, and she took the furthest, dragging herself over the bridge and plunging into the queue. Once in the carriage, she pressed herself flat against the upholstery and prayed for the wheels to move.

Joe arrived on the platform, his fine paid, and shoved his way on to the nearest train. He loped down the aisle, his eyes flicking from side to side, but they met unfamiliar faces. And Eithe saw him pass by, less than two metres between them.

'Shit, shit, shit, shit,' she said, and grabbed an abandoned newspaper and used it as cover.

Joe swept from one end of the train to the other, clambering between the seats, catching people glancing blows with his hands as he pushed from headrest to headrest. He left a wake of disgruntled passengers behind him as, realising his error, he swore, exited and took the steps of the bridge in threes.

The resonance of the engine fell to a bass snarl. Eithe heard the warning ring as the doors locked and then he was at the window. They were eye to eye on either side of the glass. The Mirror Man overlaid the other man's features, so Eithe saw two faces, one sick, the other savage.

Joe slammed his fists on the side of the train in frustration, but drew back as it started to move.

22

Chase

JOE TOOK THE NEXT TRAIN going in the
same direction.

'Why were you running? You can talk to me if you
want. It's good to get things off your chest,' said his
shadow. 'You can trust me. You know how you can trust
people only as far as you can throw them? Well I don't
weigh anything, so you can throw me quite far.'

He didn't hear her.

'There was someone else on the mountain,' whispered
the wisp. 'Someone else. Not you. Someone somewhere
else, someone not – not entire. Not whole. And
he's angry.'

His knuckles were hard on the shoulder of the chair in front, and he stared straight ahead, into the future that lay out of sight, where the rails carried over the rim of the world. He was racing his fate against Eithe's chance. The wheels pelted on.

23

The Surface Tension
of Cold Water

THE TRAIN TO SALZBURG WAS full, so Eithe and
the Mirror Man couldn't speak. And when they transferred
to Zurich, the sheer enormity of the main hall aborted any
conversation. Eithe sat down on the shiny floor and put
her back against the wall. She stared at the moving lights
of the Nova as a quarter of a million people filed past her.
None of them showed any interest in the huge LED array
as it morphed and pulsed.

'Eithe, do you want to talk?' said the Mirror Man. 'I
don't want to be quiet right now. I have to talk or I'll just
keep thinking about… things. Bad things.'

But Eithe's brain was closed for business.

'How could he possibly have known where we were? You haven't told anyone where you are going. The only map we have is my journal. The only plans we make are the online bookings, and they're ad-hoc— Hmm.'

Eithe said nothing.

'Don't bluescreen on me,' The Mirror Man said. 'Not now.'

'You're wanted,' said Eithe, because she didn't want to think about the other thing. 'Did you know about the fraud?'

'Maybe I did. I don't remember.'

'What did you do,' she said. 'Really, what did you do?'

'I used to work with the big commercial banks, maximising their investments.'

'You were a speculator. Why didn't you tell me that?'

'We aren't exactly a popular species at the moment, Eithe. I didn't want to risk alienating you before we'd made the contract.'

'I read your finances. You did pretty well out of it.'

'Yes.'

'You gambled.'

'An informed gamble.'

'That you lost, that left you in debt, and then you were given hundreds of billions of pounds of public money.'

'It wasn't just me. It was a failure of the system.'

'And you still have your flat, and your car, and your credit cards, when I couldn't afford a mortgage after years of study and work.'

'Yes,' said the Mirror Man. It wasn't an apology or an admission of guilt.

'The police probably shut down your accounts. So why does the Casey Jones card still work?'

'It doesn't link to a British bank,' said the Mirror Man.

'Offshore,' said Eithe.

'It's legal.'

'So you're a tax dodger as well. You take and you give nothing back.' Her tone held synthetic disgust and recycled rage. It wasn't real. 'You don't get to tell me what to do any more. I am not your mule.'

'Okay,' he said.

Eithe lapsed back into standby mode as she bought a ticket to anywhere and climbed onto another train, sitting mute until it reached the end of the line.

Interlaken sprawled pretty and lazy in its mountain seat. Eithe paid a euro to vomit in the station toilet, and then she sat at a bus stop in a wide open square and watched water fold over a stone plinth. Shoppers ducked in and out of the hypermarché, laden with bulging bags. The mountains were immense teeth grinding up from the ground, sharply defined against the cyan sky. The clarity of their form was shockingly beautiful.

The place made her nervous, with its wide streets and sparse population. She couldn't hide behind the bulk of buildings or in the bustle of a crowd. She joined a queue. 'What are you waiting for?' said the Mirror Man, from behind the bus shelter graffiti.

'The bus.'

'He won't have followed you here.'

'I can't stay,' she said, afraid someone would remember her height, her hair, her skin. A bus pulled up and she swung herself through the hydraulic doors.

The sun strobed as it shone between scrubby little trees. Between the skinny trunks, she spotted the glitter of water and disembarked. In the distance, mellow-brown cattle mowed the short grass. She heard the clunk of the cow bells. The water lapped against the little stones on the shoreline. The surface was smooth. She approached the edge of the lake as though she was going to stride straight into the water.

A fibreglass kayak was beached on the shingle. It hadn't been used for a long time, autumn leaves had fallen into the foot well. Eithe glanced around but there was nobody to be seen. She shrugged her coat off and dropped it on to a rock.

'What are you doing?' said the Mirror Man. Horrible chemicals pulsed through her blood as she tipped the boat to drain out the water. 'Eithe, have you used one of these before?'

'No,' she growled, as she pushed it out to the brink.

'Then don't use it now. It might not float.' She put a foot in the cockpit and the little boat dipped, pulling her off balance. 'Eithe,' he said, as she wobbled, risking her second leg. 'Don't fall in. The water is freezing cold. It comes from the glacier. If you fall, you'll struggle, and then your legs will go numb and your mind will go numb and then your heart will go numb and stop.'

'I am already numb. Perhaps I want to stop. And that would be good for you, wouldn't it? Because then there would be nothing holding you here. You'd just twang back to your body like an elastic band, problem solved.'

'It won't work like that,' he argued. 'I'd just be outside it again, trying to get in. Please don't…'

She sat down and launched clumsily by thrusting her feet against the little stones in the shallows. When she paddled with her hands, she felt the chill rising from the surface of the lake. It was not water. It was ice that had decided to move.

The kayak split the surface like strange green glass. The wind smarted her cheeks and she breathed hard. When her fingers ached too much to carry on, she wiped them on her trousers and slumped back against the low backrest. The sky was a blue-and-white bowl.

Eithe floated.

'You were so strong on the mountain,' he said.

'I can't do this,' she said. 'You're dying, and only I can stop it, and I don't know how, or why, or anything.'

The Mirror Man said, 'Well, you have to learn how. Keep moving. God, I want to shake you, but I haven't got any goddamn hands.'

'No,' she said, in a very small voice. 'I don't want to keep running. I don't want to fight.'

'Eithe,' he said. 'Life is a fight, and you can dodge, or run or hit back, or you can stand there and get punched in the face. That's it.'

Eithe wondered what it would feel like to sink down to the pebbles and mud at the bottom. It would be like lying on a freezing bed, she decided, with a mattress that would slowly suck you down and hold you and close over your head. For a cold instant, the idea was appealing.

'I don't want to be alone anymore,' she said.

The boat circled. The breeze died until the surface was smooth. 'Eithe,' said the Mirror Man, his voice like the slap of liquid on the hull.

'I can see right through you', she said. 'You're only as solid as a dream, only as deep as the skin of water.'

'Yes.'

'I'm thin too – my life, I mean. Sometimes it's like I'm not really real. My mother died giving birth to me. She had a haemorrhage.

'Dad didn't tell me how I got my name for ten years, although I asked every day. When people asked, I said it was short for Ethiopia. Then I found the note. She couldn't talk when they asked her to name me. My dad kept her final message and named me from it. She probably meant to write something normal, a name for a girl and a name for a boy. But she didn't finish the word "either" so I ended up being Eithe—'

Eithe rolled onto the backrest and looked up at the clouds.

Her hands still hurt, so she opened her shirt and thrust them inside. They felt as dead as frozen meat under her breasts. The pull of her diaphragm was uneven. It would be so easy. All she would have to do was tilt her hips and she would smash through the Mirror Man and spill into the water. Perhaps she would shut down before her lungs started to hurt. Maybe, before the end, it would feel warm.

'Tell me about your father,' he said, as if he knew what she was thinking, as if, while they spoke, she would not fall. The boat rocked like a dangerous cradle. It was a scratched and grubby white, like a shard of polar ice that had gathered dirt as it floated south.

'I don't want to.'

The Mirror Man said nothing, but it was a waiting silence.

The peaks were huge, the sun bounced off their sugar-powder caps, and in the high distance parachutists looped through the air. Eithe did not see them. The water beneath her echoed with depth.

'I phoned my dad the evening Joe proposed,' she said. 'He sounded so happy. I said I'd see him on the weekend, because I hadn't visited for a long time.

'The hospital rang three days later and said they found him in his easy chair with his hand on the phone. He just put the handset down and died. He wasn't old. Maybe his heart broke because he knew I was leaving him. Perhaps he'd been waiting for years for someone else to look after me so he could just go. He thought Joe was a good man. So did I. I didn't know.'

'Is that what it's all about?' said the Mirror Man. 'All the fear?'

She said nothing.

'Eithe, you didn't murder your parents.'

'No. But I am alone.'

The air played with her ponytail. Some of the cold lifted itself out of the lake and soaked into her trousers and socks. She pulled her fingers out of their covering and sat up. Little waves hit the kayak sideways on and it bobbed. The lake wasn't green-blue now. It was granite-grey and tipped with foam.

She spoke in a low voice. 'There is always a choice. Yes and no. So half the time, you will be wrong. And it's even worse if there are more. The more choices you have, the more likely it is that you will make a mistake.

'My mother – she was a very definite person. She very definitely didn't trust medicine, so she died. Because of her choice, I grew up without her. Why did she think what she was doing was right?

'I know Joe. He'd forgive me if I went back to him and apologised, I know he would. Joe is lanky and raddled and stares at people a bit too long, but at least he loves me.'

The wind was whipping at the water, churning the reflected world into fragments.

'Then go back to him,' said the Mirror Man. 'Maybe he'll hurt you. Maybe he won't. But we both know what's likely to happen.'

'But how do I choose? I live with a man who damages me, who controls me and won't let me out to celebrate my own wedding, or I live alone with no love at all. I want to be loved. I want what Romilly and Juliette had, what my mother and father had.'

The kayak yawed and bounced over a wave. The air was waking up. A great green wave was racing toward her. She leaned back and the little boat rose, just enough. She was wet to the waist. Her legs were useless.

Suddenly, she didn't want to be immersed. She didn't want to feel the water press her ribs into stillness. She didn't want to sink down to the point where the sun gave in and left her.

Eithe plunged her hands into the water and heaved. The surge picked her up. The kayak climbed the slope and the nose slid into the peak. Foam spurted, the droplets pricking like cold pins against her skin, but Eithe mounted the wave and all of a sudden she was over it.

The shore was a little closer, but now there was another rising wall of water, and after that another, and she didn't have a lifejacket. If she was thrown from the boat, she would fall through the Mirror Man, his lucent hands grabbing and grabbing, useless as she pierced the surface and went down.

Eithe fought the wind and the waves. She would not sink and drown. She would not die in the dark. Her breath came out in great ragged gusts with every heave of her arms. Her shoulders burned and her hands were no longer there. Soon her torso was wet with sweat. Then the lake bed rose and the plastic bottom of the boat scratched against driftwood and grit.

Eithe stood up. She splashed straight through the shallows. Her stiff fingers found the red rope and she hauled the kayak up the mud, her knees shaking, fighting the way the nylon hurt her palms.

'Good,' the Mirror Man said, as she panted. 'You're doing really well.' She dropped the boat and fell to her knees, dragging herself up the shingle and onto the grass. 'Take your jeans off,' he said.

'I thought you weren't going to tell me what to do,' she said through chattering teeth. She struggled with the zip, her fingers crooked like peeled frozen prawns. Her legs were mottled as she rolled them free.

'Your coat is over there. Put it on and spread the trousers on the rock in the sun. Try to keep warm.'

She did as he said and huddled beneath the material. She brought her shaking hands up so she could see the Mirror Man watching her from the diamonds on the ring. 'I've lost everything,' she said. 'I left the bag in the hotel.'

She heard his words reach out as though he wanted to put an arm around her. 'You have your valuables and my money,' said the Mirror Man. 'And you have me, whether you like it or not.'

'And I have this.' She pulled the little book out of her breast pocket. It was mostly dry. 'I'm glad you're here,' she said. 'Even if you are a liar, a thief and a cheat.'

Serious Fraud

KEANE SLAMMED THE PHONE DOWN and swore. The swearing went on for a very long time. Then she dialled again, for the fourth time. It took an age for anyone to answer.

'Josh,' she said. 'Thank God. Why the hell did it take you so long to pick up? Oh, that bloody, bloody game. Where's your brother? Okay. No, I'm just stressed, that's all. Look, I love you. Give him a kiss from me. I'll be home soon.'

She returned to the office. Some of the tension had gone from her shoulders.

'Eithe has unlucky friends,' said Keane, as she pulled up a chair.

Erwin, who was poring through a spreadsheet, adjusted his spectacles. He was proud of them. He'd worn them so long they'd come back into style. Privately, he hoped Keane would notice and comment on them. He knew she was in the middle of a messy break-up, possibly a divorce. But she disappointed him.

'Her colleague is in intensive care. Coincidence?'

Erwin waited. He knew his partner well enough by now to know when she was thinking aloud and needed an audience.

'The attack was after she left the country. So it wasn't Miss Dord. No contact between Dord and Imai's company and his, except the usual six degrees of separation you get in business-to-business transactions. But Dord has a small circle of acquaintances. Bit odd. Too odd. Maybe someone is trying to get to her.'

Erwin nodded and tried not to wince when his colleague's breath atomised between them. She had abandoned the Red and Green diet while they were on the road and turned to Atkins for the short term.

'We should bring her in. This time we'll try to keep her.'

Dreams Undone

JOE SAT IN A CAFE and stewed. He could have put out his arm and taken hold of her ponytail, but he missed by a slice of air, and she'd faded away. He thought about determinism and cause and effect. He ordered sweet black tea and regretted it, because the continentals couldn't brew a good cup.

'What are you drinking?' said Gemma.

'What I always drink,' he said.

When the cup arrived, he watched the way the leaves stained the fluid, the way the colour moved with the convection of water molecules, and he saw the work of encoded physics. He thought about picking up the spoon and stirring it but, even if he interfered, it would be because a particular set of circumstances led to him having that thought. Everything that lay ahead of him, from singeing his taste buds because he was too impatient to let the liquid cool, to the outcome of his chase, was pre-set, predetermined, inescapable.

He knew there was something wrong with him. A normal person would not bash a woman he barely knew half to death, and a normal person would not follow his fiancée halfway across a continent. He knew this, but he couldn't stop it. Maybe it was a faulty gene, or a medical imbalance, or the fallout from his childhood, or a noxious combination of everything, Joe didn't know. It didn't matter. It meant it wasn't his fault.

'Why do you always drink the same thing?' said Gemma.

'Why do you always want to talk?'

All he'd ever wanted was a nice life with a nice wife. Next time, he promised himself, she wouldn't have the chance to get away. He picked up the cup, sipped and burned his tongue.

Crux

IT WAS ONLY AN HOUR and a half on the train until they reached Bern. Even after the wide spaces of Interlaken, it wasn't an intimidatingly huge city.

Eithe's jeans were damp, so the Mirror Man guided her to the Westside shopping mall, a sun-sliced building that looked as though it had been glazed by a cubist. They passed Tommy Hilfiger and H&M and Tally Weijl, an unfamiliar shop which assured Eithe through its posters that 'It's fun to be sexy!'

'Oh, come on,' he said, after her third revolution of the central galleries.

'I'm choosing,' she said and, perversely, took another ten minutes to deliberate before she bought a backpack, sensible Gore-Tex boots, combat trousers and a camo-pattern stretch top. It suited her in an unexpectedly aggressive way.

Eithe rested and breakfasted at an internet café, where she took advantage of the free Wi-Fi. It was almost empty, so she risked speaking in a low voice to the screen. 'Where next?' she said, after consulting the scrapbook. She opened the next page and found a strange memento – a tiny chip of glass secured to the paper with a thick blob of glue. It glittered with microscopic flecks of copper. It was labelled 'avventurina'.

'It's Murano glass from Venice,' said Eithe, after she searched the word.

'Ah, good.'

They caught a fast train out of the city, and, once the carriage was suitably quiet, Eithe murmured to her companion.

'Why did you choose me?'

The Mirror Man said, 'I couldn't tell you. But I feel better when we talk. I feel less alone.'

'You aren't on your own,' she said. 'I'm here. It's the simplest sum. You are one, I am one. One plus one equals two.' She smiled. It was a cold smile but he returned it.

'Life isn't an equation, Eithe,' he said gently.

'No,' she agreed, under her breath. 'It isn't. With an equation, you can check and double check. You can rub it out if you're wrong. You can't do that in real life.'

'It's Joe, isn't it?' he said. 'That's what you're fussing over now.'

'If I escape him, then I'll be alone. If I go back to him, then I'll be hurt. It used to be that simple, but not now.'

'No?'

'No, because there's another variable.'

There was a strange, strained silence.

'And what's that?'

'You,' she said.

The Mirror Man's face tightened.

'Maybe,' she said, dreamily, 'I will stop searching for your identity. Maybe I'll go back to Britain and keep you with me.'

'What about our contract?'

'It isn't about that anymore,' she said. 'It hasn't been for a long time.'

'You can't stop,' he said. 'I'm dying.'

'Perhaps. And if you die, you will stay around me forever, and I'll never have to be alone again.'

'I'm a person,' he said. 'I'm not an invisible friend. You don't even like me.'

'I stayed with a man who hit me rather than be lonely. At least you can't do that,' she said.

'Eithe,' he said, desperately. 'You have to keep going. You can't just keep me.'

'I don't have to keep going. You can't make me.'

She folded her hands in her lap and thought about numbers. They allowed her to enter a quiet, pale blue zone with no shadows. The Mirror Man did not try to rouse her as she sat in her self-made calm, but he did mutter, 'Just how broken are you, really?'

A Mantle of Shadows

JOE HATED THE RED-LIT WINDOWS. He hated the way the women looked at him, speculating, evaluating, weighing him up. He had six hundred euros in cash, and he knew exactly what it would be spent on.

A herd of drunken stags crashed past him, beers in hand. Joe watched them resentfully. He hadn't been to a party since the week before he'd left for university, and he barely remembered that. He would like to be able to go to parties, but he was afraid to. Amsterdam was too much like a big celebration, with the sweet herb smoke and the shouting and the sloshing litres of beer.

He wasn't sure what he was looking for. He'd approached a number of suspicious-looking characters

with shadowed eyes and low-pulled hoods, but to
his annoyance, they'd all been polite and offered him
directions to the Anne Frank house. So he let fate take
his feet.

'Where are we going?' said Gemma. She was dyed
ruddy by the bulbs of the bordellos, running behind Joe
like a puddle of blood.

'I want to find a criminal,' said Joe.

'Why would a nice person want to talk to one of them?'
said Gemma.

'I'm not a nice person.'

'You are. You learned sign language to speak to deaf
people. You drink ethical tea. You worry about the world.'

Joe thought about the years he'd wasted trying to
be good. He'd tried so hard. He'd changed what he ate,
what he wore, how he lived and refused to buy a car. He'd
boycotted everyone from Nestlé for aggressively selling
formula to Third World mothers who mixed the powder
with infected water, to KFC for using paper made from
the ravaged rainforest. He'd campaigned, complained and
refrained. He'd licked envelopes until his tongue was desert
dry, courted hypothermia at protests, been knocked off
his bicycle during the Critical Mass rallies and his zero-
carbon commutes.

'None of it made the slightest difference,' he said.

'It did,' said Gemma. 'It made a slight difference, a little
change. Little changes add up to make big changes.'

Joe thought about the stone hitting the skull.

'I am a terrible man. I have done terrible things. I'm
going to do more terrible things.'

'But why?'

'Because I have no choice. Because there is no such
thing as choice. We have no power. The only reason we

think we have is because we're too stupid to be able to understand the machine we're living in. Everything is set. We just can't see how until it's happened.'

'What happened to you?' said Gemma. 'Why would you think that way?' He turned down a side-street. 'Don't go down there,' Gemma berated him, her scolding sharp as high heels on cobblestones. 'It's dark down there. Don't go. They'll hurt you. I don't want you hurt. I hate seeing people hurt.' She sucked at his shoes, trying to slow him, so he walked like a cinema-goer across a sticky floor.

The alleyway was dirty and dismal, and it was not on the beaten track. If he'd been alone, Joe might have died in it, or woken up hours later, stripped and battered on a bed of bin bags, his wallet, phone and papers stolen, with his teeth broken. Instead, Gemma saved his life.

'Come away,' she said, as a mother might to a toddler approaching a blazing fireplace. 'You don't need to do this.'

'Yes I do.'

The men saw him before he saw them. They were conversing in a knot, but at his arrival, they squared their shoulders, and killed the conversation. They looked like crooks, with gold teeth and corded muscles. One peeled off from the little group, his shoulders wide, his hips swaggering, toward Joe. This was the kind of person he'd been searching for.

'No,' said Gemma, panicking. 'No, just walk away! You want to, and you can, if you want to!' She hauled at him, scraps of shade clinging to his arms and his hems, but she was weak. He shrugged them away and walked on. Insubstantial fingers swiped at the uncovered skin of his hands and throat, clinging, streaking across his nose and face like a pall of dark tissue. He shook himself free of the soft, trailing fronds and swallowed hard. It was up to fate, he told himself. Whether they ignored him or attacked him or sold him what he wanted, it was up to fate.

'Hi,' he said. The word hung, tiny and foolish, in the air.

Joe was thin, tired, English and stuttering, a waiting victim – except he was wrapped all about in shadow. In the depths of the umbra, they saw their own darkness reflected, and they thought: this is not a man to mess with. So they didn't beat him up and take his belongings or just laugh at him, which would have been the worst thing they could have done. Instead, they nodded, recognising their own.

'I want to make a purchase,' said Joe.

The Sinking Maze

EITHE'S BEDROOM WAS BEAUTIFUL. THE Venetian
woodwork was resplendent with swirls. There was a
television which beamed high-pitched, frenetic-fingered
Italian soap operas. The lagoon-blue silk on the wall
flexed beneath her touch. She bathed in lavender in a
suite complete with shower caps and shoe polish in a
little basket.

'Eithe,' said the Mirror Man. 'What about
our contract?'

'It's not as important as having someone. Mmm,' said
Eithe. She sank into the bubbles. When she came up
again, he was waiting for her.

'Eithe, you can't do this.'

'I'm not doing anything.'

'I won't let you stop,' he said. 'I won't let you go back. I have some power. I'm not completely helpless. I might have no body and no way of stopping you using my money, but I still have words.' Eithe said nothing. 'If you keep me with you, they'll think you're a madwoman chatting to the glass,' he said. 'You won't have friends, because they'll be afraid of you.'

'I won't talk to you when other people are around,' said Eithe.

'Then I will make the rest of your life a misery. When you're with other people, I'll say the most terrible things to make you flinch. I will shout insults at them from the spit in your mouth. When you're alone, I'll scream until you go crazy. When you sleep, I'll whisper horrible things to give you nightmares. When you look someone else in the eye you'll see me staring back, hating you.'

'It would still be better than being alone,' said Eithe.

'Then I will be silent,' he said, 'for the rest of forever. I won't speak a word to you. I won't even look at you.'

'You can try,' she said, 'but it's not in your nature. You'll always have something to say.'

He sealed his lips.

'Fine,' she said, rolling over in the bath.

When she brushed her hair he said nothing. When she climbed into bed he said nothing. When she said goodnight, he said nothing. As she slept, he desperately stabbed at the inner surface of the smartphone, but it took no notice.

In the morning, she rose and left.

Venice was a labyrinth of canals, arches, sun-baked piazzas and little alleyways which wound out and around and back again. She paused beneath the shadow of a

church where a white-robed priest looked askance at
her bare ankles, and at market stalls which dangled with
Murano glass trinkets and food sellers whose tiered
fountains dribbled melting ice onto slices of glistening
coconut. The steps were worn to curves by the feet of
traders and tourists.

The city was fragile, unreal, cramped and winding.
Sometimes, the stale water stank. Someone nudged
her aside to take a photograph of a smoking *vaporetto*
as it chugged under the bustling bridge. Someone else
grumbled as she trod on their feet.

Alleys gave way to waterways where weed whisked
lazily in the backwash of a motorboat. Lather collected
where the water laved against the stone. The Mirror Man
sat within the scum, his eyes averted.

She walked slowly, stretching her limbs out deliberately,
savouring the freedom. She'd never walked anywhere
just for the hell of it before, she'd never explored for her
own sake.

When she'd walked for long enough, she returned
to the hotel and prepared for her ablutions. If she was
disappointed by their lack of interaction, she didn't show
it, except that later, she stepped naked from the shower
and dropped the towel on the plush carpet. He did not
comment, despite the provocation.

'I like it here,' said Eithe. 'I might just stay.' He turned
away, so her last waking memory was the improbable sight
of the back of his head reflected in the television.

As soon as her breathing became deep and regular, The
Mirror Man started working on the phone. A thin streak
of her finger-grease gave a clue to the access code. His
movements were deliberate and methodical.

At three am, he finally managed to unlock the handset.

RHIAN WALLER   143

'At fucking last,' he muttered. 'Now see who has the control.'

He explored the functions of the phone, riffling through the empty address book, testing the interface. His expression was eager and greedy as he opened the internet browser. But when he opened the email folder, he paused.

'Shit,' he said. 'I can't fucking remember anyone. Shit!'

He flicked between folders, his movements fast with frustration, until his eyes alighted on the latest message, the confirmation email from the hotel.

'Strange.'

He tracked back through them, moving from Venice to Bad Gastein to Würzburg and Paris. Since she'd bought the phone, Eithe had made several bookings, but she hadn't opened any of the auto-response emails. Nevertheless, they were marked as read. Another intruder had already been through Eithe's inbox.

The next day, Eithe dawdled aimlessly across the sinking city. Laundry wafted from lines strung between the buildings. An old woman wearing a navy head scarf shouted a warning and slopped a bucket of suds out of her back door. Little brown birds alighted on chinks in the plaster, on the rotting wooden beams that thrust out overhead, on the wrought iron bars set into the windows.

Eithe came out into St Mark's Square, an expanse of pale stone bleached by the sunlight and weathered by frost and floodwaters in the winter. Vast flocks of pigeons wheeled and settled, navigating the pillars and perching on the shoulders of tourists and the sills of palaces.

'I will find a way to make you speak again,' she said, to the cheap ring. 'I miss you. Even your bitching and criticising.'

The Mirror Man's back remained persistently stationary.

Neither of them saw the man on the other side of the square. He was tracking, his head turning right to left and back again like a radar receiver, methodical and calm, despite the confusion of faces and noise.

'How will you know your wife if you see her?' said Gemma, strong and stark in the direct sunshine as she rippled over the ground.

'I know her,' said Joe.

'You've already got an idea of who you want?' she said.

'I know exactly what I want.'

'I never really wanted much,' the shadow sighed. 'I only wanted someone with a sense of humour, who could pay his own way and wouldn't be too possessive – the usual thing. But even that seems a lot to ask, sometimes.'

'Shut up,' said Joe. 'I'm trying to see her.'

'You're very intense,' said Gemma. 'Don't you ever just want to play?'

'Play?' he said absently.

'Yes,' said Gemma. 'Have fun. Like this…'

And the people parted, naturally and spontaneously, obeying some unwritten pattern of crowd dynamics. The movement would have revealed Eithe to Joe and ended their journey. But Gemma slid under a flock of jostling pigeons, and in a moment of mischief, she threw her murky arms open and brought her hands together with a mighty clap that sounded like cracking rock.

The hazelnut-brained pigeons took flight all at once, their fanning wings obscuring Eithe. Joe jumped back, startled by the sudden detonation of feathers and claws. Gemma giggled and danced over the flagstones.

'Stop fucking around!' Joe said.

The shadow sobered up, but a dozen curious faces had turned to him with varying degrees of concern and amusement. He felt the pull of the weighty metal in his pocket. He wanted to slide his hand around it and stop their smiles, but he forced the feeling down and sidled away. Eithe glided on, unconscious of how close she had come to a lethal kiss.

In the evening, Eithe ate tender venison medallions at a lavish restaurant, ordered a bottle of Italian red, a sumptuous praline dessert and every side order on the menu. She left much of it, despite dutiful years of cooking up left overs and recycling with Joe. She was trying to aggravate the Mirror Man into complaint, but he didn't rebuke her for the expense.

'Goodnight,' she said. 'I bet you thought I'd crumple in less than an hour, didn't you? I've surprised you, haven't I?'

Outside, the moon swelled like a pregnant belly sketched white and waiting in a black satin sky. She slept soundly. On the third day, Eithe was tucked up safely in bed, sleeping because she had nothing better to do.

She woke up feeling shapeless and thirsty, her brain tightened in its cradle of bone. She emerged and bought a drink and a slice of pizza from a street vendor. She drifted into the park and sat on a patch of bare earth, her head shaded by leaves, the roots of a tree wandering past her and into the soil.

'You don't have to keep giving me the silent treatment,' she said. 'I haven't decided whether to stay or not yet, either way.' When he didn't respond, she shook the bottle so it fizzed. He still said nothing. She pressed her back against the trunk and closed her eyes.

'Venetian dogs have pissed where you're sitting,' said the Mirror Man, nastily, but she didn't flinch. 'And for as long as you're deciding whether or not to stay, then you're staying, so the decision is redundant.'

'I'm glad you're speaking to me again,' she said.

'I'm not,' said the Mirror Man.

Eithe dozed beneath the boughs, her dreams spiced by the laughter of children, and dappled by the movement of leaves. The light left by degrees, the brightness of the grass dulled, the air went blue and she felt the night on her skin.

'Good evening, sleeping beauty,' said the Mirror Man, from her ring finger. 'Did you enjoy your nap? Don't worry about me. I'm only dying, after all.'

'I'm only just starting to live,' said Eithe. 'Maybe we'll meet each other half way.'

'I was watching for you,' he said, hastily. 'I'd have woken you if anyone came too close.' She ignored him and extracted herself from the foliage.

She started back to the hotel. Venice by night was a different world. The lights glittered on the canal, bright flashes on black. The streets were still thronged with people, but in the dark, with her vision dimmed, Eithe heard the night noises with astonishing clarity. Scraps of laughter filtered from the alleyways and the wash of little waves sounded sharp and silvery.

As she passed a jetty, she heard the slosh of a gondola sliding back toward the mooring post. Two middle aged couples climbed out of the boat, giggling and teasing. They were a bit drunk, and one of them turned to Eithe and said, 'Where's your beau, honey? It's a lonely walk all by yourself.'

Eithe smiled at him, but she didn't mean it.

Fleeting Sightings

GEMMA SOUNDED FAINT IN THE twilight, as she was slowly absorbed into the greater shadow cast by the earth turning away from the sun. 'I hate this time of day,' she said in a tiny voice, as Joe paced over the Rialto bridge, cresting it again and again, shoving and pushing at the half-obscured walkers. 'I feel myself fading.'

Joe ignored her. The faces were becoming hard to read, but he thought he'd sense Eithe if she passed by. He felt sleepy, half drugged by the city, half mad and hopelessly lost. Some unconscious part of him resonated with the history of the bridge, of centuries of suicides who'd thrown themselves from the side, of the victims mugged and rolled over the wall and into the slow water.

'When you go back to the caravan, will you leave the light on all night?'

'Strange to find a shadow afraid of the dark,' murmured Joe.

'You know your wife,' said Gemma.

'I thought I did.'

'She's a real person, isn't she? I thought you were looking for an ideal but, actually, you know her already. What do you like about her? Why did you choose her?'

Joe replied with slow irritation. 'Have you ever asked anyone why they dislike peanut butter? They will say it's because it gums up the top of your mouth, or because of the texture of the grains, or because it is too salty. But if you ask people why they like peanut butter, they will say the same things. No one explains why they like or dislike something, all they do is describe it. No one really knows why they like something.'

'Oh,' said Gemma, taken aback. 'Right.'

They patrolled together, the shade and the searcher. And then, the shadow stopped. Joe slowed too. It was as though the friction between his feet and the floor had multiplied a dozen times. 'I can see something,' she said.

'You can't see,' said Joe, pulling against the suddenly glutinous pavement.

'Not here. In the outside. There's never anything in the outside, but I saw something.' Then, 'Yes,' she said. 'It's him.'

'It's her,' said Joe.

He could have run to the balustrade and targeted her as she drifted along the pavement, but his muscles had hardened with shock. By the time Joe thought to put his hand in his pocket, there were too many bodies between him and her. He struggled across the bridge, dodging a stall festooned with gilt edged masks and quills, and leaned over the other side.

His mind was a battleground of elation and a rising vapour of futility. There she was, and there she went, fading like a breath in the wind, and he had done nothing. 'Who is he?' he growled, as a boat puttered away beneath them. 'Who was he? The other man you saw?'

'I don't know!' said Gemma.

Joe kicked the wall in frustration, jerking her leg like a puppet limb.

'You said he was on the mountain that day. Tell me what you know.'

'Not much,' said Gemma, composed despite his temper. 'He wasn't happy. I don't think he was all there. But that's changing. He's – I don't know. More of a person now.'

'I will murder him,' said Joe.

Dark Canals

EITHE AND THE MIRROR MAN walked past an old
merchant's house, magnificent and ruined. Mildew crawled
up the sides and the wall was crumbling at the water line.
The Mirror Man's face, flickering half-white, half ebony in
the lantern light, was solemn.

Eithe passed a stall strung with masks. One caught
her eye.

'Who's this?' she asked, of the mournful clown.

'Pedrolino,' said the Mirror Man. 'He's sad because he
is in love with someone who does not love him. He is a
fool. He writes his poems and he moons around and stares
into the stars, all for Columbina.' Eithe turned the moon

face with its moulded tear over and over in her hands. He seemed familiar.

'He's from the Commedia Dell' Arte. Pedrolino was a zanni, a lover, a prankster, the butt of jokes, an innocent, a vengeful soul, an errand boy, an artist, an honest servant and a trickster. Columbina – she's the one he wants – will not have him because she loves the Harlequin.'

'Then they aren't meant to be together,' said Eithe.

'I don't think there is a 'meant'. A good man makes his own fate. A strong man chooses his own path.' He drew a deep breath. He held it for so long that Eithe worried he would faint before he expelled the stale air through his nostrils.

Then he said, 'How often have you told yourself you can't do something, and don't – and therefore make yourself right?'

'All the time,' said Eithe.

'There's no such thing as a perfect partner. They'll argue with you, betray you, wound you, try to define you – and you will do the same to them. But there are flaws and there are flaws,' he said.

'You're talking about Joe,' said Eithe. She replaced the mask and walked on beside the water.

'Beware Pedrolino and the anger of the clown,' said the Mirror Man. 'All he has is his fantasy. He is water and his longing is the vessel that holds him. He folds around her like a shroud and she shapes him. He wouldn't give that up if he could.'

For a moment she hated him for the tinny texture of his words, for his sardonic lilt. A great flame of self-righteousness ignited in her breast, and it burnt her shyness to cinders.

'Why do you have to be such an arse?' she snapped.

She crouched and struck the surface of the canal and broke the emaciated image of the Mirror Man into bits.

Back in her hotel room, she opened the windows wide to let the air flow. Then she sat, dejected in her bed and drank a glass of bittersweet limoncello. The Mirror Man looked out of the television at her. 'You've decided to stay,' he said, in a bleak, small voice. She shook her head.

'Eithe,' said the Mirror Man, relenting. 'Tell me, why did you choose Joe in the first place?'

'I told you. I didn't. He picked me.'

'But you chose not to say no.'

'I didn't know I had a choice at the time,' said Eithe. 'I'm not beautiful, or clever, or interesting. He was the only one who wanted to cherish me.'

'Who told you that? He did? Don't you cherish yourself? No,' said the Mirror Man. 'You don't, do you?'

'I'm sorry for hitting you.'

'I didn't feel it. I don't feel anything here, most of the time. There's something in my throat, back in England. I feel that, sometimes.'

'We're going east,' said Eithe. 'There's nothing here for us. Don't give up. Not yet. Don't fail yet.'

'I won't,' he said.

She didn't sleep. Instead, she worried about Juliette, estranged from her parents. She worried about Gerhardt, what he thought of her, and whether he had found someone else to help him with his spreadsheet. Most of all, she worried about Joe, and where he was, what he was doing, and what he was dreaming, if he dreamed at all, or if he lay like her with his back hard against the bed, his face to the ceiling, his eyes webbed with red and hurting with tiredness.

With superstitious fear, she tried to turn her mind to other things, in case, by some supernatural means, her thinking about him would lead to him thinking about her. She shuddered and reached for the phone. She flicked through the BBC front page to distract herself.

'Anything going on in the world?' said the Mirror Man.

'People are dying in Syria,' said Eithe. 'Part two of the phone hacking inquiry is still on hold. Um, Silvio Berlusconi got done for tax fraud. Does that make you feel nervous?'

'Is this relaxing you?'

'No,' she said, and put the phone away. When she finally fell asleep, she dreamed about something heavy and female waiting for her, as cold as stone, arms sheared off at the shoulders.

In the morning, The Mirror Man was waiting for her when she washed her face in the bathroom. She felt a sudden sweep of nostalgia for her own face, but when she looked up, he smiled. His lips were cracked and anaemic. 'Go on,' he said.

She walked to Santa Lucia station and, as she was buying the ticket, a policeman arrested her.

31

Sharing Shame

JOE DREAMED OF LYING IN a tacky slump in a hot and cramped room, his spit flavoured with tequila, whisky and vodka. He'd drunk far too much and was wedged with his head against the radiator and a cock drawn on his cheek. He felt soft cloth against his face, and his quasi-open eyes picked out the movement of an arm and the blur of a face.

'Don't worry. You'll like it.'

It was a woman's voice, and woman's fingers on his fly, and a woman's hand around him, tugging. He lay, addled, his senses awash in a sea of confusion, not sure, not wanting, but unable to get his tongue to work. And then she squatted over him, and slid him in, her insides wet and gripping.

'No,' he managed, 'I have a girlfriend,' and she laughed. *Laughed*, and didn't listen.

And then she'd gently raped him.

He woke with vomit in his throat. For one short, lovely moment, the world was clean and then he felt the aftershock of shame and violation. He curled up on the camp bed, not sticky and sore, as he had been, but still dirty under his skin. 'Nothing could have stopped it,' he told himself. 'It wasn't my fault. There was no choice.' It didn't occur to him that she, whoever she had been, could have chosen not to touch him.

'Stopped what?' said Gemma, as she stretched out beside him. He didn't answer. Instead, he checked it. He felt safer with the weapon in his hands.

He'd felt it burning in his bag as he tracked her. Each border crossing was a trauma, and he was braced for arrest, but no one went through his belongings. No rubber-gloved official found it. He pulled it out and turned it over and over in his hands. Then he stowed it away among the dirty socks. He lay on his side and surveyed the wall.

Eithe had been so blank and unsoiled. He'd liked having sex with her, because it felt as though he was putting the pain and humiliation into her, and she had just soaked it up. But it always came back, later. He hoped, when he caught up with them, Eithe and her man, and he burst his skin and made a hole right through him, she would know, completely and utterly, how serious he was. And if she still laughed, and ran away, or refused him, he would do the same to her. And the indignation, all the impotence he'd tried to pump into her, would blow her away. And it would die with her.

'Whatcha thinking?' said Gemma, from beneath his head. He levered himself from the pillow and flapped his hand against his head to ward away the itching. He got up and paced the room. 'Chill out,' she said. 'You're making me dizzy, marching me round like this. Left right, left right.'

'Why are you always so cheerful?' said Joe.

'Because I want to be. It's easier than being miserable.'

'That's logical.'

'I don't know why you're so concerned with logic. Life isn't logical. You look for reason, but life has no reason. It's not rational.'

'You can quantify or qualify everything,' said Joe, 'if you know all of the variables.'

'Why do you think that?'

'Because reality is what it is.'

'But reality changes. I mean, I wasn't always a shadow. Was I?'

Interrogation

THEY'D STRIPPED HER OF ANYTHING metal, even the ring. Keane sat on the other side of the desk, watching Eithe levelly. The interrogation room was not as nice as the one in Switzerland. It was small and smelled of damp and stagnation. The plaster sloughed off the walls, leaving great scabs, and the window was tiny. Eithe felt oddly calm as she rested her wrists on the table. They hadn't put her in handcuffs.

'So,' said Keane.

'So,' said Eithe.

'Conspiracy to defraud. That could be up to ten years.'

Eithe nodded.

'That's not a problem,' she said. 'I haven't tried to defraud anyone.'

'Your fingerprints were all over documentation. Anonymous papers, connected with the fraud. Suggests otherwise.'

Eithe shrugged. 'Anything you want to tell us?'

'Not really.'

'Miss Eithe, er, I mean, Miss Dord, this is a serious offence,' said Erwin. 'You don't seem like the type of girl to get mixed up in all that.'

'I'm not,' said Eithe. 'I'm not a girl.'

Keane glowered. 'Someone has been hurt. Does the name Gemma Imai mean anything to you?'

'She's my friend from work,' said Eithe. A chill went through her. Gemma wouldn't have implicated her. She couldn't have. Why would she?

'Well now she's your friend from the hospital,' said Keane. Eithe's horror was visible on her face, but the policewoman didn't modify her tone. 'Do you know why?'

'No!' said Eithe.

'Eithe,' said Erwin, who was as pale as she felt. He looked sideways at his colleague as he spoke and edged away as though she was sculpted from primed plastic explosive. 'I'm sorry. We're just concerned. We think Miss Imai may have been targeted because of her association with you. We know you have no living relatives…'

'And not many friends,' said Keane. 'Almost as though you didn't want anyone to get too close.'

'Gemma's hurt?' Eithe said. She was lost, all of a sudden. Her carefully constructed calm swirled into chaos.

'She has suffered a severe brain injury,' said Erwin. His manner, his comb-over and old spectacles reminded Eithe of her economics tutor. She stifled a hysterical giggle at the thought of her querulous lecturer strong-arming her into a police van. 'She is in a critical condition. Why would anybody want to hurt her?'

'I don't know,' whispered Eithe. Then she rallied. 'Why do you think it has anything to do with me?'

'The attack took place in her flat. They knew where she lived. She let them in. Nothing was stolen. It was a deliberate act,' said Keane. Eithe stared at her fingers. She couldn't think of anything to say. Keane made a sound that was halfway between a sigh and a snarl. 'Back to her cell,' she said.

'Eithe,' whispered the Mirror Man. 'You can't let them keep you here. I feel – you need to hurry.'

'How long will you hold me here?' said Eithe.

'As long as it takes,' said Keane.

'You can't,' said Eithe. 'What about habeas corpus?'

'We can charge you. And we will extradite you under a European Arrest Warrant. That'll speed things up. You might be back in the UK in a few days.'

'They can't take you back,' said the Mirror Man. 'It's the wrong direction. It'll waste time, and time is killing me.'

'Are you going to arrest me?' Eithe asked.

'Depends on how cooperative you are,' said Keane. 'We'll let you think it over. You might remember something helpful.'

And Eithe was escorted back to the tiny cell, with its rusty bed and the shit-stinking hole in the corner. There was no sink, she noted, and no toilet paper. She needed to relieve herself, but she decided to hold it as long as she could.

'You can't let them take you back to England,' said the Mirror Man from the cracked tiles as the door cranked shut behind her.

'What do you expect me to do,' said Eithe. 'Tie the bed sheets together and abseil out of the window? Do you happen to have baked a file in a cake? Will you dress in drag and seduce the guards? Or shall I just hope there's a dog in the corridor that I can trick into carrying the keys to me?

'Gemma is in hospital.' Eithe heard her voice winding up to a pitch of stridency she'd never used before. 'And they think it's because of *me*!'

'Isn't she just some girl in work?' said the Mirror Man, puzzled. 'You've never mentioned her before.'

'She's my friend!' Eithe snapped. 'Do you know how few of them I have? She's my friend.' She sat on the bed and hid her face in her hands. There was a knock at the door. Eithe looked up. This was confusing. She hadn't watched many cop shows – Joe had donated the television before everyone in work started talking about CSI and Dexter – but in the ones she remembered, the police didn't knock before entering the cell. It was Erwin.

'Miss Eithe?' he said. 'The police outside are saying you're talking to a man. You gave up all of your personal devices on signing in, so you have no phone.'

'Yes,' said Eithe.

'Are you okay?'

'Yes,' she said.

'Er, okay. Well, if you think of anything, please let me know.'

Then he left her as alone as she could be. Eithe waited until his footsteps faded away before she turned to her fellow prisoner. Then she rasped at him. 'You remember more than you say you do.' The Mirror Man's face was the colour of rancid cream and bisected by a hairline crack in the tile. 'You know one way we could get out of here fast?

You could just admit it. Tell me what you know and I'll tell it to them.'

'There are things,' said the Mirror Man. 'But they're personal.'

'You've seen me naked. You watched me as I slept. You replaced my face. How much more personal can we get?'

'Shhh, or he'll have you committed, and we'll never get away.'

'Maybe I should let them take me home,' she said. 'Perhaps I should give myself up to the due process of law. It would only take what, a year? And that would be long enough for you to die. *Were you involved in fraud?*'

'I—'

'Do you know how much time my company spends mopping up messes? Do you understand how much it costs people like me?' Even in an undertone, she wrapped her words around a knife-blade of controlled fury.

'I wasn't,' said the Mirror Man. 'I wasn't involved. It was only the offshore account. Accounts.'

'Oh well that's just fine then.'

'I don't want to go back,' he said, and for a moment he sounded vulnerable, like a sad little boy begging not to be sent to an unpleasant boarding school. 'I mean, all I'll be able to do is wait and watch my body die. We've got to carry on.'

'I have an idea.'

Back in the office, Keane stirred an instant coffee with the end of her ballpoint pen. The *poliziotto* behind her winced and rolled his eyes.

'How long do we wait?' said Erwin. 'I mean, how long does it normally take for them to, er, break.' He pronounced 'break' as though it was a swearword.

Keane took a sip. 'Different for everyone. But the sooner the better. Sooner I can get back home to the kids.'

'And Mr Keane?' said Erwin.

'Not him.'

Erwin suppressed a smile. Keane started filling in a Sudoku. Erwin turned to his books. Neither of them were expecting the announcement. A *poliziotto* strode in and said, 'The girl, she wants to speak.'

'That was quick' said Keane. 'Haven't even started the sevens yet.' Eithe was sitting calmly in the interrogation room. She didn't flinch when they put the recorder on. 'Right,' said Keane, once the formalities were over. She folded her arms and waited.

'I want to talk to you,' said Eithe. 'But I'll need a mirror.'

'What the fuck are you doing?' the Mirror Man whispered from a bead of sweat on Keane's temple.

'Why?' said the policewoman. She wiped the perspiration away.

'As an *aid memoire* sort of thing. It doesn't have to be anywhere near me.'

Keane pressed her lips together hard, but indicated for the prop to be brought in. One of the younger officers provided a shaving mirror. Eithe's heart was thudding as she took it. 'Come on,' she said. 'Into the glass.'

'You're fucking *batshit*,' said the Mirror Man from beyond the frame.

Keane said, 'Are you ill?'

'Trust me. They won't just let us go. This is the best way,' said Eithe.

'No!' said the Mirror Man. 'Shut up, for Christ's sake!'

'Some people can see you. Maybe they will.'

'Jesus!'

'Okay, enough of this,' said Keane.

'Do it!' said Eithe.

So, reluctantly, the Mirror Man edged into the mirror. Eithe held it up and twisted so they could see the aberrant reflection. Then she looked back at them. Keane was positively thunderous, but Erwin stared into the mirror, transfixed. 'It's a bit too early for an insanity plea,' said Keane. She took the mirror from Eithe's hand. 'Unless you have something useful to say, then it's back to the cell.'

Erwin's mouth hung open very slightly.

They escorted Eithe back to the room and locked the door behind her.

'And what good did that do?' railed the Mirror Man, as soon as it shut. 'Now they just think you're stupid or nuts, or playing games. What if they think you're messing with them? They'll think you really do know something. We'll be on a plane before you can cough and they'll drag me right back with you. Shit. Shit!'

'It was a gamble,' said Eithe.

'It was stupid.'

'It wasn't that stupid,' she said, hotly. 'Remember in Paris? Juliette saw you. She thought you were my 'male soul' or whatever. And people keep giving me funny looks. I think Erwin could hear you.'

'You could have told me. If you'd given me time to think, I could have told you what to say.'

'And what would happen then, when I knew about all of your dodgy dealing all of a sudden? They'd think I was in on it, and there'd be no chance of them letting me go.'

The Mirror Man lapsed into strangulated grumbling.

Then the little panel in the door slid sideways. Erwin and his spectacles looked through. 'There was a man,' he said. 'Blaspheming.'

'I call him the Mirror Man,' said Eithe.

'That's unusual.'

'Yes.'

'You won't, you know, strangle me with my tie or seduce me if I come in.'

'I promise I won't,' said Eithe solemnly.

'Right.'

The door was unlocked and Erwin sidled in and perched on the edge of the bed. 'Detective Inspector Keane isn't happy,' he said. 'She's trying to find something to charge you with to keep you longer. Obstruction or withholding evidence, I'm not sure which.'

'I honestly can't tell you any more than I already have about the fraud,' said Eithe. 'But I can try to explain why I'm here.' And she told him as calmly as she could about her flight, about Joe and about the Mirror Man.

'There are people who can help you,' said Erwin. He took off his glasses and buffed them with his tie. 'With the situation with your fiancé. I don't think there's much we could do unless you came back to Britain. But I can give you numbers for a domestic abuse line if he continues to harass you.'

'I'd like that,' said Eithe. 'But the most important thing now is for us to leave.'

'Can I – can I talk to him? I brought this.' Erwin pulled a spoon out of his pocket. 'It's all I could think of.'

'You might have to sit behind me,' said Eithe. She accepted the piece of cutlery and he repositioned himself so that he could see the Mirror Man, inverted and distorted by the concavity of the shallow spoon.

'Good afternoon,' said Erwin.

'You need to change your hair,' said the Mirror Man. 'It'll start flapping in a strong breeze.'

'I heard him again,' said Erwin, more fascinated than offended.

'Look, we don't have time for you to be all amazed and in denial,' said the Mirror Man. 'It's very important that you let us go. I'm dying. I can't remember much, but I think if I do start remembering then I'll know how to go back to my body and wake up. If I don't, then I die, and whatever information I had, well, that ends up rotting. Then we're both fucked. I'm searching for something – anything – that will help me remember myself. When I find it, I'll come back to you, and I'll tell you everything I know. I promise. You can keep my body as a guarantee.'

Erwin was new to the job, but he was obviously no fool. 'You'll tell me,' he said. 'You come to me, not Scotland Yard, not Interpol.'

'Just you,' said the Mirror Man.

'Right,' said Erwin. 'Come on then, while Keane is busy.' He hurried them back to the desk, had them discharged and hastily handed back the confiscated bag and phone. 'Go,' he said. 'Fast. And if you have another account, a secure one, then use it. We have a trace on Casey Jones.'

'Thank you,' said Eithe.

Erwin watched her leave. Then he casually returned to the staff room where he picked up his copy of *American Gods* and started reading.

When Keane came in, blistering with rage at the incompetence of the police force, he looked over the pages and said, 'I let them go. We'll have to go back to England and wait for him to wake up. At least you'll get to see your kids. And by the way, would you like to go for a drink some time?'

33

In the Attic

NEITHER EITHE OR THE MIRROR Man paid much attention to the pretty buildings or bridges as the train pulled away. 'They said they had a trace on me,' she said. 'Do you think Joe could as well, somehow?'

The Mirror Man said, 'Well, it's not like we're leaving a papertrail.'

'No,' she mused.

The Mirror Man made a sudden involuntary grunt, as though he'd just forgotten, or just remembered, something inconvenient.

'There's only – oh,' said Eithe.

A suspicion started growing in her mind. It was muddled and misty, but she waited and willed it to take form. But before the realisation coalesced, the Mirror Man interrupted. 'The emails,' he blathered. 'The only person who knows where you are—'

'Is Juliette,' said Eithe. Her face was dour. She ground her jaw.

'Are you okay?' said the Mirror Man. If guilt tickled at him, and he pushed it away, Eithe failed to read it in his eyes.

'You can't trust anyone,' she said, her voice held hard to stop it wobbling. To distract herself, she leafed through the journal. 'Your next clue - it's a postcard of a place called Rijeka. That's not far.'

They crossed the border into Slovenia in just a few hours, and then changed lines. The livery of the carriage was muddy and the inside was battered, brown and smelled of smoke. As the engine tugged away from the platform, they entered a different, less luxurious Europe. At Rijeka, the train coughed, shunted forward once and died.

The Mirror Man gave Eithe a reassuring wink from the window. She looked through him. Men were running up and down the platform, shouting. Some were in overalls. The people around her started to grumble, and a conductor arrived to usher them off.

'This is right. This is it. We should stay here for a bit.' He added more quietly, 'Because at least that way, no one knows where you are.'

On one side, Rijeka was a jumble of flats, high-rises and older four-storey buildings rising out of the trees on the hill. On the other, it was a mass of cargo ships and warehouses, towering cranes and sea mist. Eithe walked past the cafés and little shops, past a wine bar which shone with sprays of fairy lights, past students walking with books in hand. A wedding cavalcade clad in mauve ribbons blared their horns so loudly they could have been mistaken for a car crash.

Eithe wandered through the Roman gate sandwiched between two much younger buildings. The main street was paved with volcanic grey blocks pounded by the feet of shoppers. She rubbed her taut abdomen and felt her bladder strain. 'I need the toilet,' she said.

'Take a McPiss.'

But when she went into the McDonalds, there was a key pad on the door. She knew they would only give her the code if she bought something.

'Just get some McNuggets,' said the Mirror Man as she tightened her legs.

'No.' The refusal tasted good in her mouth, dry and crisp.

'I bet Joe wouldn't let you,' he said. 'Because of McLibel or Supersize Me or because some vegetarians ate beef fries.'

Eithe steeled herself. 'Joe is full of shit,' she said. 'And he's a psychopath. But that doesn't mean he wasn't right about some things.' Then she left.

The Mirror Man sounded grudgingly admiring when he said, 'We should find you somewhere to stay. There's a guest house on the front. Just go toward the port and follow the shore.'

Wind scattered salt across the road. A tanker on the horizon sank into the dark smudge of the sky. Light sparkled over the little waves at the edge of the ending day. In the foreground, the sea sucked at the wall and in the middle distance cranes moved thirty-tonne cargo crates like toy building blocks.

The guest house lay where two roads pinched together. It was tall and triangular and its walls were plastered orange. Bits of it were rotting and the fence was weather-gnawed and rusty. Green shutters clashed with the crumbling walls. Plants that had outgrown their pots sat on the roof and flung their leaves over the guttering.

Eithe knocked on the door. Nobody answered so she knocked again. The third time, she gave up and decided to head back in town and find a hotel, but the door opened behind her. A quarter-face looked through the gap.

'Oh, hi,' she said to the one curious eye and a slew of curls. 'Do you have any rooms spare?'

'Yes.'

The door was caught on a hand-woven rag rug, so it took a few attempts to open. A dumpy woman with a kind face and a dated floral dress stood panting on the other side. 'Thank you,' said Eithe, as she stepped over the threshold. 'Where shall I put my bags?'

'Up and up again.'

Eithe climbed the stairs two at a time, discarded her luggage and ran to the bathroom on the first floor. After a while she emerged and took the squeaking staircase up to the attic room. There was a bed, a chest of drawers, a portrait mirror on a freestanding frame, an old telephone and not much else.

'What are you doing?' asked the Mirror Man as Eithe reached for the phone.

'I'm going to call him.'

She dialled anonymously. There was a click.

'Hello?' said Joe. Eithe held the receiver so close to the side of her head that her ear hurt. 'Hello?' Eithe opened her mouth but nothing came out, and she couldn't remember any of the words she'd rehearsed to herself, as righteous and truthful as they had been. 'Listen, this is costing me money. I'm hanging up,' said Joe. He sounded tired and reedy over the poor connection. There was an echo on the line.

'Wait,' said Eithe.

'You,' said Joe through the sound of cracking ice.

'Me,' said Eithe.

'Where are you?'

'I'm not saying,' said Eithe. She was surprised by how firmly she spoke. 'You need to tell me something. Did Juliette let you know where I am?' There was white noise. 'I need to know for sure.' Eithe waited. Then she said something that surprised them both. 'Joe, I'm sorry.'

'So you did do it.'

'You mistake me,' said Eithe, and the words unlocked themselves and came more easily. 'I went out that night, and I'm not sorry for that. I'm sorry you think you need me. I'm sorry you feel so strongly. You can stop now.' A snowstorm blew out of the earpiece.

'I don't want you to make a decision right away,' she said. 'I know how it feels. It's like standing in the middle of the crossroads and not knowing which road to take and all the time the traffic is coming faster and faster until you know you have to move, except that there is danger everywhere. I understand.'

She waited.

'This is the longest you have ever listened to me,' she said.

There was no reply. Eithe had once read that the hiss over the airwaves was the sound of entropy. She stood and listened to dying stars, red shift and the expansion of the universe.

'Joe?'

'I am going to hunt you down,' said Joe at last. 'I'm sorry. I have no choice.'

She slammed the phone onto its hook. She wondered if, through the cheap engagement ring, the Mirror Man could feel the capillaries in her fingers drain with shock. He was observing her from the red curve of the receiver.

'Are you okay?' he said, after she'd stood for a few breaths.

'Yeah.'

Eithe lay down on the squeaky bedstead in the bare little room and dozed. She woke when he stroked her forehead with a cool hand. She opened her eyes.

'I'm here,' said the Mirror Man. She smiled at him because she could not speak. She rolled over and studied the sinuous line of his spine. Her lips moved soundlessly on his neck, spelling out a question.

The flux of his breath lifted the loose strands of her hair. He rolled away. Eithe's arms stretched as she tried to keep contact, but their skin snapped apart. He scratched his arse as he shuffled along the corridor and into the bathroom. Eithe heard his urine gush into the toilet pan.

He didn't come back.

She called for him, silently.

'Eithe,' he said. 'I'm not really real.'

The toilet flushed. Eithe slid off the bed, wandered down the corridor and pushed the bathroom door open. He was in the shower. She could see his silhouette rippled by the folds of the curtain. The pool of water pushed under the hem. The flood crept further and further out, spreading until she stood in a puddle.

'?,' she mouthed, worried now.

The shower pattered. She lifted a cautious foot, came closer to the curtain. With a trembling hand, she drew it aside. His back was turned to her, cold and dripping.

'!,' she tried to shout, but he twisted, turned, changed, and suddenly it wasn't The Mirror Man at all. It was Joe, skinny, naked, wet and vicious, and his hands were out and his lips were wide and they closed over her mouth and nose like a seal. He sucked the air from her lungs and she felt her ribs squeaking as they rubbed against each other, caving into her chest. She tried to scream, but her throat was shut and airless. Pale arms snaked and squeezed around her poking shoulder blades. Her spine bent under the stress of angry muscle, snapped, collapsed.

When he let go, she was just a skin hanging in his grip. He shook her out to flatten the kinks and wrinkles and folded her up like a sheet. Her staring eyes went blind as he tucked her soft head into her belly and used her lax arms to tie her up into a neat little parcel.

'Hey.' The voice was sharp and selfish. 'Hey!' It sliced through the dream like a newly stropped razor.

Eithe woke up. Her mouth felt dry and unsavoury. 'Oh god,' she said.

It was sunset and the birds were moving. She heard their skinny little feet tapping on the corrugated roof. She had only slept for a few moments. 'I didn't want to wake you,' said the Mirror Man, with the all the virtue of remorse. 'I thought you needed the rest.' She looked at the skylight and he looked down at her. His face was mean with strain and shrunken with worry, and it was not the one she had imagined, but she was still glad to see it.

'You saved me from an evil dream,' said Eithe.

'It's getting dark,' he said.

'It's time to go looking,' she said.

'You know,' he said, 'you're a woman on your own. Perhaps it isn't such a good idea for you to go into the grimy parts of town.'

'It isn't a good idea,' said Eithe. 'But I'm going to do it anyway.'

'Eithe,' he said, and then he seemed to change his mind about whatever he was going to say.

She never found out if it was going to be advice, confession or argument, because she said, 'You read about it all the time, coma patients waking up after sleeping for years. Do they all go wandering like you?'

'Who knows?'

'Maybe,' she said, dreamily, 'they are all out there too, with you. Perhaps you'll meet them and introduce them to me.' A chill rolled through her, like wind from the mountains, but it was the Mirror Man who shivered.

'It's a big space out here,' he said. 'It goes on forever. If there is anyone else, I doubt I'd find them.'

'Isn't it funny?' she said. 'You're probably in hospital right now, and that's being funded by tax-payers. And you didn't pay tax. You'd be dead already if it wasn't for the rest of us.'

'Please, Eithe. You're making me feel strange.'

'I think you mean 'guilty',' she said.

She showered and dressed in muted colours. She felt like a thief as she went down the stairs and out into the dusk. Eithe was distant as they followed the sea wall, blind to the movement of the city.

'I remember the beach down there. I sprayed something on the wall. Maybe it was my name,' said the Mirror Man.

Eithe went down a flight of weed-slick stairs which led down from the pavement. It twisted at right angles and on the low wall, she saw two words.

'Is this it? Is it my graffiti?'

She used her phone to illuminate the tag. It read: 'Try Fly.'

'No. They must have washed it off.'

She continued down to the concrete-cupped beach. Something about the curve of the coast took away a lot of the power of the sea, and the little peaks and troughs of Kvarner Bay sank down into bubbling frills which caressed the shingle.

She sat on a rock. A young couple had spread a coat over the smaller pebbles and were cuddling in the evening murk. They hadn't noticed her.

A ship's horn blared in the distance. The moon shone magnolia through the threadbare clouds. 'What are you thinking about?' the Mirror Man murmured.

'Nothing,' said Eithe.

'You are,' he said.

Behind her, the girl uttered a little needy noise.

Eithe left the beach. There was a blockage in her throat. She hurried along the sea wall as a mist rolled in, swallowing up the road ahead and behind, her sleeve over her nose to mop up the moisture. When she came to the guest house, she shouldered the door from its swollen frame and rushed through the kitchen, up the stairs and into the bedroom where she curled up on the quilt.

'Eithe, what's wrong?' said the Mirror Man.

'I'm afraid,' she said.

'You haven't emailed any- Juliette,' said the Mirror Man. 'He won't find you here.'

'I'm not afraid of that. I'm afraid that - I can't.'

Eithe looked at the stained ceiling.

When Joe had reached for her, she hadn't minded. He was her fiancé, which was almost a husband, and a husband and wife were supposed to have sex. It was just something they did. He would rub her nipples and bite her earlobes and then he would push himself in and, after the first few times, it didn't hurt. There was only the displacement of her flesh as he moved in and out. When he came, she could sleep.

'Joe used to ask if it was good,' she said. 'I always said yes. I think he asked because he needed reassurance, not because he really cared.'

'You lied,' said the Mirror Man,

'Yes.'

'It really bothers you, doesn't it?'

'Yes.'

'You've never tried it out yourself?' said the Mirror Man.

'No,' she said. 'Nobody ever taught me how.'

The Mirror Man chuckled. It was a dark, throbbing sound.

'I can tell you.'

'No,' said Eithe, with abject mortification.

'It's up to you,' he said.

She turned the light off to cover her blush. In the darkness, she thought about Gerhardt, about want, and need, and thirst, and purpose and disappointment. She pulled the covers between her legs and clasped them tight. 'Tell me,' she said.

'Okay,' said the Mirror Man. He was quiet for a few moments, and Eithe, waiting, felt a blend of acute frustration and fear.

'Well?' she said.

'Do you know your own body?' he said.

'I – I don't know.'

'Then touch it,' he said. 'First your face. Use both hands.'

She brought her palms over the planes of her skull. It felt simultaneously familiar and alien, and she struggled to remember what she looked like. Maybe she'd needed to see herself, she thought, to remind herself that she had a solid shape, but perhaps touching would work just as well. Her nose was still her nose; her lips were still her lips. Her jaw curved into her neck, a bone edifice above a pillar of muscle. Her fingers found the soft dent of her clavicle.

'Further down,' said the Mirror Man.

She slid between the weight of the covers and her breasts.

'Further down,' said the Mirror Man.

She felt the eagle-wing sweep of her ribs and the tender flesh of her abdomen, wandered over the dent of her bellybutton and stopped.

'Further down.'

'I can't,' said Eithe, the motherless child, the girl who avoided the excruciating pastoral lessons by hiding beneath the table, her nose in a maths book, who found out about menses when she woke to a bloodied brown bed sheet and thought she was dying, whose father sat her down and asked if she had any questions, and was so embarrassed she said, 'I don't know'.

'It's up to you,' said the Mirror Man.

She lay with her hands splayed over the narrowing triangle of her hips. She felt the coarse hair trickle beneath her fingernails. She stopped when her parting flesh made a faint liquid noise. 'What now?' she said, her breathing uneven.

'Move your fingers as though someone was kissing you,' said the Mirror Man. 'Pull with them and then slide them inside. Pull them out slowly and then push them back in. Imagine a tongue touching and tasting you. Imagine—'

His words fused with her thoughts, until she wasn't sure if the low, slow instructions were entering her ears or emerging from her mind. Eithe felt the fluttering, tiny at first and then stronger and stronger, drawing her into herself. Then she relaxed so utterly that she didn't know whether she would draw another breath.

She didn't think the Mirror Man had heard her climax. She was utterly quiet until she roused, left the bed, picked up the mirror, laid it on the pillow and then settled down next to it. Her breath glazed the glass. 'Thank you,' she said.

'You're welcome,' said the Mirror Man.

They lay, nose to nose, cheek to cheek. 'Do you want to know who I thought about?' she said.

'No,' said the Mirror Man after a while.

'Why not?'

'Because I think I'd be jealous,' he said.

She leaned over and set her smiling lips to the glass. It was not a quick kiss.

'Goodnight Eithe,' said the Mirror Man.

'I wish I knew your name,' she said. 'Then I could say goodnight to you properly.'

'I think you just did.'

Eithe let out a happy little sigh.

In the faint light of the streetlamp, the Mirror Man watched her eyes move beneath their lids and felt remorse gnaw at his guts.

When she woke the next morning, her arms were around the mirror. He was as close to his side as she to hers, and he looked rested although he was not asleep.

She stretched and blinked blearily.

'Well,' she said.

'Well,' said the Mirror Man.

'There's nothing for us here.'

When she peeled herself away, the gap opened up between them like a void. The imprint of her face stayed on the glass.

'I should look at your book. Wait there.' She rolled out of the bed and walked naked to her coat. She unzipped the poacher's pocket of the waterproof, where she kept the journal.

'Keeping it close to your heart?' said the Mirror Man.

She returned to the bed to peruse the pages. Turning the next one felt like opening the window of an Advent calendar. It revealed a pressed cutting from a pine tree. It was brown and squashed in a plastic wallet. There was a little label attached to it, reading: 'Mt Vitosha, Sophia'.

'I'll check the times,' said Eithe, reaching for her phone and twisting onto her back. 'I can book the train online.'

'Eithe—' said the Mirror Man.

'Yes?'

'There's something I should have said earlier.'

'Yes?'

'—I just wanted you to know that if I said something that hurt you, or didn't say something I should have, well, sometimes things go too far and too much time has passed to correct it. But I know that, out here, it's only me and you. I've only got you.' Then he closed his mouth.

Eithe smiled at him.

'That's okay. You can thank me when we've set you free.'

Three minutes later, the confirmation email dropped into her inbox.

The Dragon Bridge

THE GREAT GRASSY PARK LED into the core of
Ljubljana. Joe was between trains, so he stalked the byways
of the Tivoli municipal park, past budding flowerbeds and
gravel strips, rows of trees and stands of bushes. People
picnicked in the morning sun. Gemma basked in the rays
whenever he paused.

A dark, tall girl with her hair pulled into a strict plait
jogged down the path. Instinctively, he froze, but it wasn't
her. A booth drew him with the promise of frying onions,
but when he saw that the menu advertised horse burgers,
he retreated, sickened.

The city centre streets were wide and clean. Crowds
waited at the kerb until the crossing lights turned green.

Joe and his shadow were in a liminal space. This was not the Mediterranean and it was not the Balkans. It was some strange blurring of the two. It was at the crook of the continent.

He knew he was getting closer.

It was unlikely that Eithe would be in Ljubljana, but he saw her in every movement, in every shop window, out of the corner of his eye when he turned his head too quickly. He tried to blink away the ghosts and walked past the candy pink facade of the church, over the left-most of the three bridges and along the river. Then he stopped in his tracks. He was being watched. It was a strange sensation. He wanted to flatten himself across the floor or hide. He looked up. There were dragons the green of corroded copper sitting on twin plinths. They regarded him with placid, reptilian disinterest.

'What is it?' said Gemma, blind but aware.

Joe experienced a sudden blossoming of fellow-feeling. He nodded at the nearest dragon with its tongue curled out of its snout, and leaned against the side of its plinth to light a cigarette. His back fitted into a scoop worn into the stone.

'Nothing,' he said. 'Just statues. Time for a breather.'

Smoke pushed out of his nostrils. Gemma sensed his pensive sadness and nuzzled the back of his neck.

'I could stand here forever,' said Joe. 'Watching, like the dragons. My stepfather used to shoot. He said that the best thing to do was not to run after the prey. You spook it. Better to build yourself a hide or stay very, very still and wait.

'He used to come back with a brace of birds, with their feathers broken and their chests blown half away. I didn't want to eat them. I wanted to be vegetarian. But he laughed at me, which was worse than shouting, and he called me a pansy. I ate the pie and picked bits of lead out of my mouth. In the end I got used to the idea of blood.

'I could wait here for years. I would get old and stooped and thin. I could come here every day from dawn until dusk with a packet of sandwiches and wear this hole in the wall deeper with my shoulder blades. I would take no one else. I don't want anyone else.

'She is going east. I could wait until she goes so far she has run all the way around the world back to me. And when I saw her again, she would be grey and tired. Perhaps she wouldn't recognise me. But I would remember her.' He lit a second cigarette from the stub of the first. The side of his mouth quirked with the start of a smile or the beginning of a sob.

'I would ask her to dance with me. I would put down my stick and I would open my arms, and we would step together in the moonlight, and we would be married. You could be the maid of honour. The dragon could be my best man.

'And while we were dancing, with my knees cracking, we would waltz closer and closer to the balustrade and I would whisper in her ear about all the children we never had, all the times we never spent together, all the years we lost. Then I would push her over the side. But I haven't got the patience. So I'm going to carry on running for her and I will catch up. I will. It is inevitable.'

Gemma said nothing.

'Well?' Joe demanded. 'What do you think?'

'I'm tired arguing and tired of your responses – "why, because, why, because, why, because". I'm tired of your refusal to be comforted and be friends. You aren't going to listen to what I say.'

Joe scraped the cigarette down the side of the plinth, scarring the shadow temporarily, and then ambled away. He stopped when his phone warbled and he picked up the email.

The
Overnight Express

EITHE FELT THE HARD WEAVE of the seat on her
bare shoulders. A thin rail-issue blanket lay over her like
a cheap shroud. A train on the opposite track shuttled
past, its wind buffeting the carriage until it rocked a
counterpoint to her pulse.

'You are thinking about Joe again, aren't you?' said the
Mirror Man, with an echo of his old peevishness.

'Yes,' said Eithe. 'I don't know if I should face him, or
go back to him, because as long as I don't decide, as long
as I keep running, it won't be done. There's nothing wrong
with running, sometimes.

'I'm going to sleep,' said Eithe, 'we're safe here, and nothing can be done while we're moving.'

She didn't know that, three carriages down, Joe was sitting in a compartment with his most recent purchase in his bag.

The train curved like a snake sliding through a pipe. Joe sat straight on the seat. His hair was a crushed mop and his clothes were stained. It was not physical strength holding him upright. He looked out of the window. There was nothing much to see. Orange and powder-yellow lights shone here and there, but mostly there were textures of darkness.

'Do you have any hobbies?' asked Gemma. She wrapped her insubstantial arms around his chest, and he did not resist. The cuddle was gentle and cool, although it was strange, with her limbs rising straight from the cushion.

'My father would have liked me to have liked football,' said Joe. He muttered, mostly to himself. 'Father would have liked me to have been anything else.'

Gemma, naturally loquacious, didn't like to see anyone descend into a black, miserable world no wider than their mind. She said, 'So, tell me about your wife. What is there about her that brings you across the Eurozone? It's a long way to go for a bit of ass.'

'Eithe is not a piece of ass.' He tore himself from the bizarre embrace.

'I'm sorry,' said Gemma. But something snagged in her memory, some shred of a former life.

Joe waved a hand. 'She's a strange girl. I didn't think that anyone else would want her, apart from me. I didn't think anyone else would see it.'

'See what?'

'No one took me seriously. No one!' his voice cracked. 'She was the only one in the whole world who believed in me. Not once, not once—' he held up a wavering finger, 'did she laugh at me. And now she is gone.'

Gemma sensed dangerous waters and gamely paddled away.

'So, Joe, do you like to travel?'

Joe shrugged. 'I would like to go to Stalingrad and Leningrad, except that they aren't called that any more. I'd like to go to Cuba, but Fidel stepped down. I'd like to go to China, but McDonalds got there first. Do you know this is the first time I've ever left England?

'We were going to go on honeymoon to volunteer at an orphanage in Romania. I never told her that, because it was going to be a surprise.'

'A modern couple,' said Gemma.

'Do you believe in fate?' said Joe.

'No. I don't.'

'I don't believe either. I know it's true. You don't have to believe in the truth to make it true. Because, see, we are not free. There's only one way I can be otherwise I wouldn't be me. And we're all like that. All of us. Trapped. Bricks in a wall. Cells in blood. We might think we are choosing, but there's only one way we can go.'

'That's deep.'

The locomotive roamed through the blackness. A sudden biological urge cut through Joe's thoughts. 'I need a piss,' he said.

A few carriages down, Eithe felt the fullness of her own bladder and pushed the blanket away. The first toilet was occupied, so she shuffled down the corridor to the second.

The lavatory well was an open hole and if it had been light, she would have been able to see the sleepers flickering past. The sink was blocked with paper. She tried not to touch anything as she hovered over the cold seat and let loose.

Joe waited outside the door, tapping his feet.

'Fucking hell,' he said.

He heard the rush of water.

Eithe pulled up her underwear and redid her zip. The lock flipped from engaged to vacant.

Eithe opened the door just as the man in the next cubicle came out, so there was a narrow plywood screen between her and her waiting fiancé, who stepped into the malodorous little space.

Unaware of Eithe's close presence, Joe splashed the bowl and staggered back to his compartment. The train lowed a warning as it crossed a bridge. It sounded like a lost creature calling in the night. The carriage smelled of sweat and long journeys.

'She betrayed me,' said Joe. 'She did the worst thing one person can do to another, except for rape or murder. She took my life and smashed it to pieces. I haven't stopped since she left. I've searched and searched. I know I stink. I am so tired I can feel my heart drying out and turning black inside my chest. But I am still going to make her mine. Until death do us part.'

'Why are you chasing for her if she hurt you so badly?'

Joe took a little while to decide what to say. Wheels scoured the tracks. The nose of the train folded the night on either side.

'Nothing is undecided. Everything is set. No one is free to choose. We were meant to meet. It was an unavoidable fate. I wouldn't have it be this way if I could. Do you think I want to care this much? Who would choose pain?'

'A masochist,' said Gemma under her breath.

Joe wasn't listening. 'I care,' he said. 'I care a lot. There are people starving to death all over the world and I care about them even though I haven't met them. I gave them some of my pay cheque, when I had one. I'm happy to pay tax to the NHS, but I don't want to give my money to the military. I want to make the world a better place. When I have her, I'll be able to. This is just an interruption.

'Why is Eithe doing this to me?'

'I—' Gemma said, but Joe wasn't listening. He'd finally stopped fighting his fatigue.

Soon deep snores started filtering up to coat the ceiling with something thick and viscous.

Gemma was made and unmade with every flash passing the window, and stayed, deep in thought, trying to hold on to the slender thread. 'Eithe,' she said, and knew it was a word she'd used herself and used often. 'Eithe,' she said again.

Some way down the carriage, Eithe slept, oblivious. She woke at dawn, her face unguarded against the light. 'We'll be there soon,' said the Mirror Man. 'Get your things together.'

'I feel hideous,' said Eithe.

'You look hideous too,' said the Mirror Man, but he was only teasing.

'Shut up.'

She left the compartment and stood with her hands on the handle of the door, watching the new country unfold.

Thousands of sunflowers beamed at her from the fields. When the train drew into the city of Sofia, Eithe alighted on the platform and strode away.

The conductor on patrol banged on the door of the compartment with the drawn curtains. Joe snorted and woke. He hurried down the corridor and staggered onto the platform before he found his balance. He was just in time to see her leave, her corkscrews bouncing, and join the clutter of people at the station.

36

Culture Shock

'WHAT ARE YOU DOING?' ASKED Gemma, as Joe
piled goods into the wire basket. He only picked up
the cans with ring-pulls and long-life milk, packets of
crisps, chocolate and bread, things you could eat with
your fingers, things that did not need cooking and would
not spoil.

'Getting supplies,' muttered Joe.

He paid at the checkout and lugged the stretching
plastic bags on to the tram. It rapidly filled with city folk
heading for the railway station, and soon he was swamped
by gently perspiring bodies. He squirmed. He was sitting
at crotch height, and, despite not having washed in a week,
it made him uncomfortable.

There was a woman jammed up against him. She wore a loose polyester top and her arms stuck out from it like two knobbly sticks. Her hair was white at the base, but dyed a violent orange, and he could see the varicose veins winding up into her skirt. She looked tired, and she was carrying even more than him. He left the plastic cup of the seat and pushed into the people, gesturing to the vacant space.

'Would you like to sit?'

He expected the woman to nod and smile her thanks. Instead, she gave him a look of utter contempt and lifted her chin. 'No?' he said, stung by her rudeness. 'Really? Fine. Fuck you.' He sat back down and smouldered.

'Well I thought it was a nice thing you did,' said Gemma.

He exited the carriage and walked back to the railway station, a huge, muscular box that, despite the addition of a marquee roof, a water feature and a bevy of little shops, could not disguise its nature. He found a bench and sat down.

A few hours later, Gemma, who had been thinking, said, 'Do I know Eithe?'

'No,' said Joe.

A few hours later, she said, 'Are we going to move on now?'

'No,' said Joe.

A few hours later, the light went.

Abandonment

THEY BOOKED INTO A HOSTEL and Eithe sat in the great hall with high rafters and cool flagstones. Around her, travellers ate pasta and tomato sauce doled out from an industrial sized catering bowl. Later, she retired to the ten-bed dormitory in a traditional Bulgarian house that skulked in a courtyard behind a steel shutter. 'I'm glad we're here,' she said, as she locked the bathroom door. 'It has more, I don't know, something.'

'Are you tired of hotel rooms?' said the Mirror Man.

'I suppose you've seen a lot of them,' said Eithe, to the looking-glass.

'Too many. Before – a long time ago, I couldn't afford them. Then it was always hotels.'

'Hostels seem friendlier.' She sounded wistful.
'Everyone seems to just hang out together.'

'I'm stopping you from talking to other people,' he said.

'I don't feel like making new friends yet. I'd rather talk
to you. How are you feeling?' she asked. He looked as grey
as a three-day corpse.

'Stable,' he said.

'That sounds like something a doctor would say,' she
said, as she stripped.

'Yeah,' said the Mirror Man.

'Better hurry then,' said Eithe.

'You need to get some sleep,' he said. 'I think we should
take the tram around the city tomorrow. I remember that.
Maybe we will find something that way.'

'Goodnight,' said Eithe.

'Night.'

'Are you still there?' she whispered, a few minutes later,
as she lay in her bunk.

'Yes.'

'Don't you get bored when I sleep?'

'I used to. I used to resent how you shut down,'
he admitted. 'I can't do that. Now I'm just glad you
sleep soundly.'

The next morning, showered and fed, she took to
the streets.

Eithe avoided one open manhole and almost fell down
another. The road was uneven and the factory chimneys
stuck up around the skyline and pumped grey fumes into
the air. She walked down a road of yellow bricks and
through a wide avenue. On one side, a huge golden dome
glinted. In one lane, long black saloon cars crawled past,
the passengers invisible behind tinted windows. A man

drove a wooden cart down the other. His horse swished its tail, dropped some dung on the road and chewed its bit.

Eithe climbed aboard a tram and swung herself onto a battered plastic chair. The tram rolled over a bridge flanked by dumb, tongue-less stone lions.

It carried her through the town, beneath a bridge, through the underpass and the wasteland patches where the trees scratched at the carriage. It turned off into an industrial zone where the souls of old factories watched through smashed windows and lizards sunbathed on broken bricks. Little plants pushed through the bitumen of the pot-hole pocked pavements. The track looped around and took her to the other side of the city. Now they could see Mount Vitosha.

'I walked up it once,' he said, as they disembarked. 'There were dragonflies beside me, following the stream that ran alongside the track. Their bodies flashed green and blue as they flew.'

Eithe picked her way over the rubble of a demolished building. There was a half-built house, the slabs of concrete and metal skeleton still naked. It looked utterly abandoned. 'This is wrong,' said the Mirror Man. 'This wasn't here. There were more trees. Maybe I sent you the wrong way.'

'I'll take a look,' said Eithe. 'If I go to the top floor maybe we'll see something.'

She navigated the stony slope, through the spiny little plants and past the hovering wasps that suckled at the tiny, brightly-coloured flowers. The pillars of the unfinished home admitted her as she stepped over the threshold. Her footsteps were crisp on the uncarpeted stairwell. The third storey was stunted, the walls only up to chest height, the sky was the roof. The flat concrete floor stretched out in front of them.

Eithe moved carefully until she came to the brink of open space. In the distance she could see the trees, but the city had taken a great grey bite out of the forest. 'It wasn't like this,' said the Mirror Man. 'It was green, all the way out. What happened?'

'Progress, perhaps. How long ago were you here?'

'Half a life ago,' he said.

'I need to rest,' said Eithe, swinging her legs over the side. The ground was thirty feet down. 'And we need to think. We're following you. A younger you. Why did you come here? Do you remember?'

'Some of it. The land, the language – a little, the weather, but not why I was here, or what I did. I hope it wasn't something pointless, stupid and unprofitable. Maybe I was here on business.'

'I don't think so,' said Eithe. 'Why would you spend time on the mountain in summer if you were working?'

'Hmm.'

'The sun will set soon,' said Eithe.

'Time to go back.'

'No,' said Eithe. 'I want to see the city light up.'

The shape of the Mirror Man, duplicated in the facets of the ring, was almost too small to see. So Eithe didn't notice a peculiar expression pass across his face. It was partly irritation and partly a strange sort of pride. 'As you will,' he said. 'I'll leave you alone, if you like.'

'Please,' she said, and so he went.

The city winked and worked beneath a pall of smog. In the dark, as she lay back on the hard concrete, Eithe half-fancied that she could hear the bristling scrub grass drinking up the scattered droplets, like thousands of tiny straws sucking at the bottom of a glass. In the undergrowth, the crickets shrilled.

'I'm ready to go now,' she said, but the Mirror Man did not reply. 'Hello,' she said, feeling as foolish as when she spoke into a dead phone. 'Hello?'

There was no answer.

'You aren't giving me the silent treatment, are you?' said Eithe. She shook the ring as though he was a goldfish in a bag, but there was no response. She held her hand up to the failing light and stared into the diamond. It was empty. There was no reflection at all. The Mirror Man was gone and he had left nothing in his place.

Then she really wanted to know his name, so she could curse it.

38

Basilisk

THE SKY WAS THE COLOUR of scar tissue. 'Please move,' begged Gemma. 'You can't stay here all night again.'

But Joe did not move, and in despair, she turned away from him and into the unreality. This time, it was not completely empty.

Dissolution

THE MIRROR MAN SAW THE shadow in the distance, although in truth there was no distance between them. He was in the non-space that lay outside infinity, so there was more of it than everything, without being anything at all.

The shadow was a dark smudge in space, shifting and shapeless without a body to give it form. But it was something, in the zero, and the revenant form terrified him. He started to run with feet he didn't have at the sudden, puncturing realisation that he was not alone.

'Hey!' he heard. 'Hey!'

It billowed, then it pulled herself into a more familiar shape. Legs coalesced and kicked as it frantically began to swim for him. 'Stop!' it said. Its words were oddly dead in the nothingness. There was no air to carry them, no acoustics to texture them, so they were as real as the words he heard inside his own skull and as loud as thought.

He struggled away from it as it wallowed, its parts fluctuating, some as dark as the heart of a thunder cloud. Its borders were translucent and badly defined. 'Don't!' it said. 'I'm not going to hurt you.'

His legs were not strong enough to carry him. There was no ground to support him, no traction to give him speed. And he couldn't, no matter how hard he tried, run any further. Even though he couldn't see Eithe, he was still tethered to her. The shadow drew closer, closer to him.

It was a monster, an apparition, something inexplicable and strange and because fear is based on the unknown, it was terrifying. It reached out and he felt himself being hauled toward it. The shadow wavered as it drew him close. He did the only thing he could think to do. He attacked.

'Get away!' he said, as his insubstantial arms pushed away at the clinging shade. It tried to scratch and snag. It couldn't get a hold on his flimsy body, which was only as solid as the silvering on the back of a mirror, the sheen of oil on a rainy road or the glassiness of a dying eye. They tangled around each other, terrified of letting go, terrified of touching, unable to do any damage.

'Calm down,' the shadow said. 'Please. I just want to know who you are. Wait, wait!'

His flailing slowed. 'Who I am?' he said. 'Who are you?' The Mirror Man started to laugh. 'I don't know who I am. Well, not a lot about who I am. Do you know who you are?'

'Not all of me,' said the shadow. 'But I did, once.' The dark, flowing limbs released their hold on him. 'I thought

I was the only one out here,' it said. 'Until I saw you. You scared me.'

'*I* scared *you*? Why?' said the Mirror Man. 'There's not much I can do to anyone like this.'

'You aren't complete. We are supposed to be whole but all you were was dread and rage.'

'Were?'

'Not now,' the shadow said. 'Now there's something else.'

They hung in the nothing, regarding each other.

'You were a woman,' he said. 'From the way you hold yourself.'

'I think so. I'm not sure.'

'How did you end up here?'

'Something hurt me, hurt my body, very badly. So I left it. What about you?'

'I –' he hesitated.

'There's nothing to be ashamed of,' said the shadow. 'We're not even really here.'

'I haven't told anyone how I ended up like this.'

'Do you have anyone to tell?'

'There is someone,' he said, and he smiled, despite himself, and the smile was audible when he spoke.

'Ah, so there's the change,' said the other, with a shadowy little smirk. 'I have someone too. It makes things easier, to know there is someone I can talk with, to comfort. He's so cynical and sad. He is trying to find his true love. Maybe if I help him, I can find a way back to my body. Is that what you're doing?'

'Not exactly,' he said.

She said, 'What's your name?'

'I don't remember. Why do you think we can't remember?'

'I suppose it's because memory is an organic thing. Our brains are somewhere over there, *inside*. And our connections are growing weaker, so perhaps the longer we are out here, the less we will know. I really miss my body. Not out of vanity, but because –'

'But because it's yours,' said the Mirror Man.

'Exactly. I don't think there's a self without the flesh. It's part of me. I'm part of it. No, that's all wrong. That sounds like two things tied together. There is no me without it. Oh, I don't know. I don't have the right words.'

'I understand.'

'Oh, it's good to hear someone say that. I miss everybody.'

'Who?' said the Mirror Man. 'I don't remember anybody to miss.'

'There must be some people. Colleagues, friends, maybe a lover. I worry about them.'

'But you don't know who they are.'

'I remember my little brother. And the others are still people,' said the shadow simply. 'Anyway, you didn't finish. About how you found yourself here. Nowhere.'

The Mirror Man kept his attention on her face as he tried to find a way to phrase his thoughts. She moved like a cloud in high wind, shifting in complicated fluctuation, and he could see her refining herself, trying to maintain contours that she was only guessing at. Sometimes her face was sharp, sometimes rounded, sometimes not even humanoid.

'I wanted to,' he said.

'What?'

'I don't mean I wanted to be here. But I did want to get away, and now I'm stuck again, but this time it's on someone else.

'I've never wanted to be tied to anyone, ever. In the memories I still have access to, I can't remember any time when I was with someone without a reason, because they would help me succeed or because they had some information I needed, or because I worked with them. I wanted to be absolute, detached, distinct, self-sufficient. And I was.

'I only remember bits. Useless bits. My desk, with a black leather chair. Shouting at someone incompetent. Lots of incompetent colleagues.' He barked out a laugh. 'I remember giving myself motivational speeches into a mirror. I used mirrors a lot. I liked to look at myself. It reminded me I didn't need anyone else, because I was always with me. Literally, by myself.

'The day I fell into the mirror, I don't remember why, but I felt fabulously lonely, and horribly tired of being myself. I remember staring into the mirror, thinking that if I could only leave my self for a moment then I could be happy. And then something happened. It felt like something picked me up and flipped me over, inverted me and then I was looking at my own face. It looked different from the outside. Smaller.

'And you know what the strangest thing was? For a moment, just for a moment, I felt relief. I thought I was free. And then I realised I'd carried my self with me. I had exactly what I wanted, and I hated it. I couldn't even escape through my body. I can't shower, I can't fuck, I can't get drunk, I can't even bloody smoke. And now I have nothing else at all.'

'Except for your person. Is it a man, or a woman, or someone else? What are they like?'

'She's a she. Some Caucasian and some African in her somewhere, maybe about five foot eleven, difficult hair, chews her lip sometimes and fiddles with her nails. She dressed plain, but now she's started wearing colours.'

'No, no,' said the shadow. 'I meant what's she like, not what she looks like.'

'Ah,' said the Mirror Man. 'She's shaky, nervous, dithering, kind, innocent and stronger than she thinks she is. I don't have an easy movie list like: "she's smart, she's funny, she's brave, she's beautiful". Maybe she is beautiful, in a way and she is funny, sometimes, and she has ways of thinking that I can't follow, which is a sort of smart, and she is kind-of brave, to travel alone with just a face and a voice for company. She is a runner, not a fighter like you.'

'What is she running from?'

'From one very bad decision she made a long time ago. There's a man following her, and she's afraid he's going to kill her. And there's me.'

'Do you talk to her?'

'Not about everything. There are some secrets I have to keep, some things she can't know.'

'And you are good to her?' The Mirror Man didn't reply at first.

'Not always,' he said.

'You should be,' said Gemma. 'She's all you have.'

'I have myself,' he said, but he didn't sound certain. 'That used to be enough. That used to be everything.'

'But not anymore.'

'Mmm,' he said, non-committal.

'You know,' she said, 'your story reminds me of something. In Japan and China, there are legends that say people are joined together from birth by a red rope. My favourite was about a rich man who was told by a seer that he was destined for a poor young girl. He was horrified at the thought of marrying someone of such a low caste, so he sent a man out to kill her with a knife.

'The years went by and he met a beautiful young woman who he fell deeply in love with and asked her to marry him. Her features were delicate and her manners were perfect, but she always wore a cloth around her head. He asked her to take it off, but she refused. He asked again, and with tears on her cheeks, she said that when she was a child, a madman had appeared from the crowd and stabbed her, but she had run away. The wound left a scar. Her husband took her in his arms and sobbed with her.

'The bond can never be severed. Sometimes it leads to a wonderful romance, sometimes to a terrible tragedy.'

'Nothing is inescapable,' said the Mirror Man. 'You can always change something. A good man makes his own fate.'

'Some things are inevitable, some things aren't,' said the shadow, philosophically. 'The trick is to know what you can change and just deal with the things you can't.'

'Very Zen.'

'Don't be facetious. Your woman hasn't been putting up with you for too long, has she?'

'Only a few weeks. You?'

'About the same. I became aware and he was there, thank God.'

The Mirror Man frowned. 'What is he like?'

'Romantic,' said the shadow. 'Melancholy, determined.'

'I mean, what does he look like?'

'I can't really see him. Not in the normal way. He's a gap in the shadows. I'm sort of sewn on to him and he drags me around like a cloak. I'm a bit tattered from where I was torn from my body.'

'My person is carrying me,' said the Mirror Man. 'I'm still attached to my body, a bit. It's like a rope on a suspension bridge. Part is knotted to my body but part is tied to her. I think that's the stronger bond. I'm holding on to her and she's holding on to me. The other knot is coming loose.

'I'm not taking anything from her really,' he said, with an edge of sarcasm. 'Except her face, her time and a space in her psyche. I'm a vampire, a leech, a cancer.'

'I'm sure you're not.'

'How do you know he deserves your help?' said the Mirror Man. 'How do you know he isn't the reason you're trapped out here?'

'What do you mean?'

'I haven't told her why I'm here,' he said, suddenly deeply abashed. 'And I don't think I ever will.'

'Why?'

'Because if I did, she wouldn't help me. It's my fault, you see. There's a reason I chose her as my host. Everyone else was closed up, whole, complete. But when I saw her, and saw how precarious her sense of self was, I knew it would be easy to displace. She was tired and scared and vulnerable. So I attached myself to her and pushed her reflection aside. All I wanted was for someone to see me. I know it was wrong. I would never have done it if I'd known there was no way back. I'm in there now, curled up in her mind, and I have to stay small in case she feels me in there. And that's why I can't tell her.'

'You could just say you are sorry,' said Gemma

'I – I don't apologise.'

'You could.'

The Mirror Man said nothing. He wondered how long he'd been away, because there was no way to tell what time had passed in the outside. 'I should go back to her,' he said. 'I've left her alone for a while. Will you be here tomorrow?'

'We move quite a lot,' she admitted. 'I'm glad I met you, but I have to stay with him. He's my only link to the world.'

'Ask him about the woman he's trying to find,' said the Mirror Man. 'If I have my secrets, then he probably has his.'

'I will,' said the shadow.

'Goodbye then,' said the Mirror Man.

'Bye.'

When he returned to the other side of unreality, it was with some relief. The dusky mountain, the first few stars and Eithe, lying on her back and breathing quietly, brought him back into the world.

He watched as Eithe sighed until her lungs were as empty as a spent balloon, and then she let go. At first he thought she was sleeping, and he waited patiently, watchful from the sliced gem. And then he became aware of her heartbeat which had become a background sensation as natural as his own distant homeostasis. It was faltering.

'Eithe,' said the Mirror Man.

She didn't respond. He had the unpleasant impression that she wasn't there.

'Eithe?'

Her mouth was slack and her eyes were open but they weren't moving. They looked like dull pennies.

'Eithe!'

Her pulse slowed.

The Mirror Man screamed, and the sound was the smashing of diamonds. 'Eithe, you're losing yourself!'

His words woke her and she slammed into her body with a sharp breath. There was a dense reverberation of thunder. Eithe shook herself like a dog. She felt indistinct and nebulous.

The ground pattered under the first heavy drops of rain.

'I'm okay,' she said.

'I know what you were doing,' he said. 'I tried to do it myself. Do you know how close you were to ending up like me? You were half-empty and the rest was leaking away. Why did you do it?'

'I thought you'd gone,' she said. 'It's been hours. I kept looking in the glass and there was nothing there. Do you know how strange that is? It was as if I wasn't real. I tried to follow you.' Eithe shivered then.

'No,' he said. 'No, Eithe. Maybe you can't see yourself, but you are very real. Honestly.'

Thunder cracked.

'Come on,' said the Mirror Man, as the rain gained weight, and in the earth at the foundations of the unfinished house, the worms began to wriggle to the surface.

She swore beneath her breath as she ran for the tram. The rain sheeted down, bouncing off the dusty road and creating a slurry that coated her shoes. She leapt onto the tram when the ponderous doors ground open. Drops splattered on the window and hammered on the roof. 'You almost went,' said the Mirror Man from the window. 'I almost lost you.'

'It was too easy,' said Eithe. 'There's so little holding me here.'

'Don't,' said the Mirror Man.

'Why?' said Eithe.

'Because I'd miss you,' he said, simply. Lightning strobed the concrete and cloud.

'True,' she said. They said nothing for some time. She leaned her head on the window, and he did the same so they lolled, brow to brow.

'Eithe,' said the Mirror Man.

'Yes?'

'About the emails. Don't write Juliette off. You don't know for sure that she's been telling Joe where you are.' She still looked worried. There was mischief in his voice when he said, 'I met someone else, on the outside. A woman.' Eithe said nothing at first. 'She was very nice.'

'So I will be seeing less of you then?' she said, with a touch of exasperation. 'Not that I'm complaining.'

'Oh, Eithe, you aren't jealous are you?' he teased.

'No,' she sulked, and he was tickled.

'There's nothing wrong with being a little bit jealous. And it's understandable, when you're talking about me. I am marvellous, clever and very modest.'

'You don't need to get any more arrogant,' she said.

He laughed. 'No,' he said, 'I don't.'

But Eithe had unstrung, the tension had faded. She was dozing and he had to wake her when they came to the stop. That night, as she settled into her bunk, he said, 'There's something you should know.'

'Yes?' Eithe was calm, peaceful and only half-awake.

'Never mind,' he said. 'It's probably not important. I'll tell you tomorrow.'

'What is it?'

'Don't worry. We've travelled far enough that it shouldn't be a problem.'

She rolled over and soon there were no more questions.

By the morning, Eithe's sleep and the Mirror Man's relief had swept away whatever would have been said. At noon, Eithe trailed toward the station, past the

regurgitating water features and the little shops selling
plastic things.

There was a tramp sitting on a seat outside the station,
oblivious to the bustling buses and taxis. The hard slats
of wood bit into his back. A beard crawled all over his
face and his belongings were his pillow. Eithe wondered
whether he'd chosen his life, or whether he'd ever known
what choice was.

He scanned the crowd, left to right and back to the left.

He was so changed, Eithe didn't know him. The Mirror
Man recognised him first.

'Eithe,' he said, 'it's Joe.'

Eithe froze, and the head stopped turning.

'Go,' said the Mirror Man. 'Go!'

Joe rose from the seat he hadn't left for thirty hours.

Eithe ran.

Joe kicked over the bottle of urine as he came after her.
His hands were raw from where he'd pinched the skin to
keep himself awake, and his heart palpitated with an excess
of caffeine, but he moved fast.

Eithe slid between bodies, the crowd a blur. She
worked her backpack from her shoulders and flung it
at her pursuer. He leaped it without missing a step. Joe
grabbed people by the shoulders and shoved them aside.
He crashed into a kissing couple. The woman reeled back,
hands to her tooth-gashed mouth.

'Hoi,' shouted the man, but Joe just whirled, his fist out,
and grouted his gums with blood.

Eithe ducked into a little alley shadowed by
jutting balconies.

Joe's heavy footsteps ricocheted off the
breezeblock walls.

She took a turn and twisted left, upsetting a dustbin with a clang and wading through sacks of rubbish. 'Get back into the street!' shouted the Mirror Man. 'He can't attack where there are people!'

She was too busy running to reply. The world turned into a series of angles, walls and guttering. She took the maze of corners without seeing, without thinking, and then she ran into a dead end. There was a window behind corroded bars and a boarded up door.

Eithe wrenched the handle. It didn't even rattle.

Joe slowed to a stroll. His shadow danced like a fish on a line. He paused, as though he was listening to a voice Eithe could not hear, but then he shook it away.

'Don't struggle, Eithe,' he said. 'You can't fight fate. Say you're sorry, you can still come back.'

'Tell him you don't want to,' said the Mirror Man. 'Tell him the truth.' Eithe threw her shoulder against the door and it tossed her back into the alley.

'Eithe,' said Joe. He sounded almost kind. 'You don't know what you want.'

'Don't I?' she snarled. Her right hand quested and found a rusty bar. She tugged and the metal flaked and groaned, but it did not give way.

'Eithe,' said Joe. 'I'm not coming back without you. Whoever he is, you're safer with me. We are meant to be married.'

The Mirror Man slammed his palms against the invisible barrier in desperation. 'Eithe!' he shouted.

Joe reached into his pocket and brought out the gun.

It had a gleaming stainless steel finish. The Mirror Man slid around the barrel. He stretched diagonally and compressed again as the muzzle dipped up and down. Eithe knew the bullet would shine as it revolved through the air and he would ride it straight into her, and he would spread in the red reflection of her blood.

Joe released the safety catch. 'No!' he shouted to his shadow. 'You can't stop me!'

'Oh God,' said Eithe. She jerked the bars and they came away and clanged as they hit the ground.

'Give up,' said Joe, and she turned to face him. 'Or I'll take you down. Shut *up*!'

'Who are you shouting at?' Eithe said. Her shoulder clicked as she twisted it awkwardly to test the wall behind her.

'I've been thinking about us,' said Joe. 'I think I was a little hard. I don't want to scare you. It's just that I love you so very much. Think what we would be like together. We could adopt a child. We could take him to the park and buy him ice-cream. I'd get a better job and you could stay at home and care for him. We could grow old and sit in the sun holding hands.'

Eithe's patting fingers found the window. They drummed against the glass. 'No,' she said, in a very small voice.

'Pardon?' said Joe.

'No,' said Eithe, stronger now.

Joe's throat jogged as he swallowed his anger. 'Eithe.' It was a low warning.

'No!'

Then he pulled the trigger.

The bullet ground out of the chamber, spiralling as it went, ripping the hot air. The Mirror Man's pressing hands found hers and her feet left the ground as he dragged her through the veil and into the void.

The lead hit the glass and it shattered in a cyclone of hail.

40

Realisation

'IT'S YOUR FAULT,' SAID JOE, low and furious. He
threw the gun at her, but it just bounced off the ground
and skittered into the bins. 'You held me back.'

'Wasn't it fate?' said the cowering shadow, her hands
over her head after the ear-ruining noise.

'Shut up.'

'Tell me about your beloved,' said Gemma, raggedly.
'What does she look like? Is she bronze and tall and more
scared than she should be?'

'Shut up.'

'She is, isn't she? She's running away. She's running
away from you.'

'You don't know anything. Stupid bitch.'

Then the shade uncoiled and drew herself up.

'Say that again.'

'I'm sorry. I didn't mean to call you a bitch.'

'I've heard that once before,' she said.

'No you haven't,' said Joe, but he couldn't convince her or himself. 'You must be imagining it. It's the shock, Gemma.'

'Gemma?' she said. 'So you do know me. And I know you,' she said, as the fog in her head began to clear. 'Oh yes I do.'

Revelation

THE VOID SUCKED AT HER eyes, her sinuses squeezed and she felt her skin strain to keep her blood in. 'Don't breathe out,' said the Mirror Man. His fingers were clinched with hers like the teeth of a zip. 'Your lungs will collapse. Don't talk.'

The space around them couldn't be called space. It was a purer vacuum than the distance between galaxies. There was no dark energy, no radio waves, nothing. Looking at it hurt because she had nothing to focus on, so she locked eyes with the Mirror Man.

She saw him reflected in his own cornea, over and over, and, without the subtle distortion of not-quite parallel mirrors, it went on forever, an endless repetition of selves leading into the pupil, which held infinite depth. She fell into it, down and down into the black, until she seized on a tiny pinprick of light. Hungry for something solid, she moved toward it, and it coalesced into a fire in a grate. Before it was the hunched shape of a weeping man, tall but bent, his dark hair flopping loose as he fed a sheaf of paper into the flames and watched the names and numbers burn.

There was a tug, she felt herself move as though she was being thrown into a spin by a dancing partner, and then she hit glass.

Eithe clawed her way out of the pane, falling out of the door dividing one carriage from the next. He'd pulled her into a train, but she didn't have time to find out where it was heading. She clambered over the people sitting on the vestibule floor, barged into the toilet and leaned over the sink.

A stream of puke hit the Mirror Man in the face. Then the diarrhoea started, and she was glad that the cubicle was small, because she could sit on the seat and keep her chin on the rim of the hand basin. The pain ripped down her belly and gut. She gasped and spluttered. Someone knocked on the door but Eithe was too busy ejecting to reply. Eventually she stopped bothering to flush. She shook uncontrollably and her throat was scalded by hot stomach juices.

When there was nothing left in her to lose, she pulled her pants up and washed her hands and face. She was utterly empty. Her brain was swimming in pickle brine. When she spoke her tongue felt like a fat caterpillar.

'All the time?' she said. 'That's what it's like, all the time?'

'Yes,' said the Mirror Man.

'That's where you're trapped?'

'Yes.'

'But there's nothing. Nothing at all.'

'No.'

'It's awful.'

'Yes.'

She put her arms around herself and rocked back and forth. 'I don't ever want to go back there,' she said.

'No.'

She looked at him, her face tearstained. 'Is that what it's like to die?' she said.

'I don't think so,' he said. 'I think when you die, you're gone. I'm still here, in nowhere.'

'You saved me,' she said, and he looked gratified and guilty all at once. Then her forehead corrugated. 'I didn't email the Rainbow,' she said. 'And he still knew.'

'Eithe,' said the Mirror Man, as understanding dawned.

'He hacked my account,' she said. The Mirror Man made a neutral noise.

Slowly, slowly, she turned to him, her face frozen. 'You – you knew.'

'I wanted to tell you,' he said, wretchedly.

'But you didn't,' she said, rage sweeping away her sympathy like floodwater spilling silt. 'You just let me carry on, with him right there behind me. Was it what you wanted?' she snapped. 'For him to find me?'

'No! You know, I could have turned your phone GPS tracker on.'

'Stop telling me what you didn't do. Tell me *why* you didn't warn me!'

'I didn't want you to stop,' he said, ashamed. 'I wanted him to make you afraid. Which is shit. It's really shit. I didn't even want him to get close. I just wanted him somewhere behind us, so we would keep going forward.

'I've carried you like a parasite from one side of the continent to the other,' said Eithe, her voice harsh with horror. 'I've gone further than I ever wanted to find your stupid soul, which, if it's anything like what I've seen of you, is selfish and shrivelled and not worth finding.'

'I know,' said the Mirror Man.

'You almost got me killed,' she spat. 'Of course you did, because your life is worth much more than mine.'

'No,' said the Mirror Man.

'Oh,' she moaned, and for a second she thought she might be sick again. 'Oh, you wanted to get free, and you were worried – you were worried you were stuck to me. You wanted me dead.'

'I didn't know he had a gun,' said the Mirror Man. 'I didn't want him to hurt you. If I'd wanted you to die, I would have told you to jump from the kayak,' he said, appealing to logic. 'Or I would have let you just float away when you were lying on the rooftop.'

'You are as bad as him,' she wailed. 'You are just as bad as Joe. I swapped one for another. Is it me? What's wrong with me that I end up with people like you?'

'There's nothing wrong with you,' said the Mirror Man helplessly. 'There's something wrong with me. I'm trying to fix it. Please, give me…'

'Tricks and words,' she said, rods of steel sliding through her voice. 'I'll find out how to set you free. But I'm not sure I'll tell you how. When I know, I will keep it to myself.'

'You would murder me?' he sounded dazed and, oddly, hopeful.

'No I wouldn't,' she said. 'I'd go back to London, to wherever you lie. And I'd tell them everything I knew and so they could keep you alive, as you are, forever. You wouldn't die, you wouldn't go back to your body. You'd just stay.'

'This isn't life,' said the Mirror Man, and the hope had gone, replaced by an almost hysterical desperation. 'This isn't life! You felt it. You know what it's like.' Eithe shrugged. 'I can't taste or touch or feel,' he went on. 'The only power I have is to keep or share what little information I've got. I had control, Eithe. You don't know what it's like to have that taken away, to feel utterly helpless.'

'Yes,' said Eithe in a small voice. 'I do.' And then with defiance, she said, 'And I never, ever used it as an excuse to hurt someone else.'

'I didn't mean to hurt you,' he said.

'But you didn't care if you did.'

'I did care,' he said. And then he was quiet as he digested his own words. 'I do care,' he said again. 'I care about you.'

But Eithe was awash with rage. 'Shut up,' she said. 'Just shut up.'

The Mirror Man said something else that sculpted an unfamiliar shape on his tongue and lips. 'I'm sorry.'

'No,' she said. 'You're only sorry for yourself. But I'll make you sorry.'

She pulled the journal from her pocket. He winced as she ripped out the first page, balled it and threw it down the toilet. Her anger was fuelled by the bitterness of betrayal, and the tang was worse because finally she'd touched him, and it had hurt. She ripped another leaf. Once down the toilet, it was blown about and pulverised by the metal wheels.

'Please don't,' he said.

'Now I know how you felt,' she said, with brutal satisfaction. 'Being in charge, withholding information. Good, isn't it?' The paper hissed as its fibres parted. Bit by bit, she fed the journal to the hole in the floor. Then she walked into a first class carriage and turned her shoulder to the window. She took off the ring and shoved it in her pocket. She put her coat over her head and ignored him.

She ignored him as she changed trains and in the café while she waited. She pretended she was alone in the coach and she stayed silent as she made the connection with another train. She still hadn't spoken to him by the time the sun set and rose again and she crossed the border into Serbia.

The train rolled through the outskirts of Belgrade. Rows and rows of tents clustered in the grim districts along the railway line. Bits of rag and plastic flapped in the wind. The sky was bullet grey behind the monolithic tower blocks. There were places around Manchester where refrigerators and cars were left to corrode. But in Belgrade, people lived where the metal things went to die.

She'd lost everything again, except for the two rings, one cheap, one antique, the phone, her wallet and passport.

Eithe's mind tumbled the same thought over and over like washing in a drier.

He knew, he knew and he didn't tell me. He knew.

The railway station was a dark concrete block. In the ticket room, the seats were made of battered wood and the tiles were scuffed. On the destination board, the times flipped and ticked as they rolled over. She picked up a tourist map from an information booth. The street outside bordered a building site. Woodchip boards lined the pavement and cars rocketed around an incomprehensible set of junctions. Eithe followed the map up the hill. It wasn't steep, but she was tired. The traffic threw up blue-black clouds of leaded petrol.

She boarded a tram and stared out of the window. 'I remember this place,' said the Mirror Man. 'If you leave at the next stop, you can find a hostel.' Eithe did not respond, but she disembarked. It could have been a different city.

Little stars sparkled in the trees. The cafés spilled out into a square and people sipped coffee and conversed under canvas awnings. Fountains sprayed spears of water which transformed from lilac to a chilly blue as the lights beneath them changed shade. Eithe went down a side street which was thronged by pedestrians. Traders sold hair accessories and trinkets on wobbly trestle tables and an artist swore as he wrestled with his easel. She found the steel-reinforced door and pressed the button labelled 3-8. There was a crackle and then a voice filtered casually through the intercom. 'Hey?'

'Oh, hi,' said Eithe. 'You take guests?'

'Sure, sure,' said someone. 'Push the door.'

The stairwell was utilitarian and echoing, but well swept. She went up to the second floor and wandered along an open balcony that overlooked the tops of red umbrellas, while above, washing lines wrote a complicated geometry across the clouds.

The door to the hostel was open. It was a little flat that had seen better decades and tried to stay there. The carpet was brown, the wallpaper was swirly and floral and the furniture was well used. A table and bench filled the front room.

'Hey,' said one of the men sitting at the table. He had a stern, corrugated bulldog face. Eithe thought he would be quite lovely if he could stop sagging for a little while. 'Do you want a beer?'

'Oh, yeah,' said Eithe. 'Please.' One of the guests shuffled down the bench to give her room. Eithe felt suddenly shy and hunched over the bottle. She drank it fast and was given another.

'My name is Javor,' said the man who had offered her the beer. Eithe decided that he was the hostel owner. 'You are from England, quiet girl?'

'Have you been there?'

'Hah, no. It is hard to leave Serbia,' he said. 'The visas, they do not come easy. Would you like me to open you another beer?'

The Mirror Man looked like a wrung washcloth, pale despite the brown glass of the bottle. 'Is that a good idea?' he said. His voice was a quiet fluting like breath over the open neck of a beer bottle.

'Yes,' she said, to Javor.

There was a whole roast chicken wrapped in tinfoil. Javor placed a loaf of bread beside it and took a bowl of chopped cucumber from the fridge. 'It is for everyone,' he said, when he saw how Eithe hung back.

It was only when one of the men, Igor, broke the bread that she realised how hungry she was. The slick chicken skin snapped between her fingers. Eithe ate and ate until her stomach bulged. 'So what brings you here?' said Igor.

'A man.'

'Is this someone who loves you?'

'No,' Eithe said, fiercely.

'Do you love him?'

There was a pause. 'No,' said Eithe, finally. 'It's strictly business.'

'You know,' said Igor, 'you sound very angry. Often you are angrier at someone you love than someone you hate.'

While the host cleared the table, Eithe said, 'Do I owe you anything for the meal?' The men stared at her with varying degrees of offended hurt. 'Never mind then,' said Eithe. She took out her handset, logged in and checked her emails. A scattering of messages let her know that Joe still cared. She opened one up.

I am going to find you and rip you apart.

Eithe sat back in her seat and glanced over her shoulder. The men were laughing and toasting and teasing each other. She told herself they were good people and that she was safe with them. Her fingers rested softly on the face of the phone.

Bonjour, read the next. *Ca va?*
   I have not heard from you for an age. Tell us of your adventures.
   Juliette

Eithe clicked on: reply, and typed:

Dear Juliette,

I am travelling with a traitor. I thought it was you. I am so, so sorry.

Then she erased the message. She was speaking to herself, not the Mirror Man when she said, 'Well, if he's eavesdropping, then I'll give him something to read,' and wrote:

Dear Juliette,

I'm on the plane. I thought I'd let you know before I have to switch off.

I'm heading home. I'm tired and I've run out of money. I can't carry on. I'll keep in touch when I get back to England. I'm so looking forward to going home.

She signed off, drew a glass of water and said, 'I'm going to bed now.'

'Sleep well,' said Javor.

Her room was carpeted in tattered paisley-patterned brown. The open window overlooked the square. Drums drowned out the sounds of late night coffee chatter and foot traffic.

The heavy clouds that gloomed over the inner city split down the middle. Through them, Eithe could see the beginnings of the sunset.

The bedsheets were bobbled from a thousand washes. She shut her eyes obstinately and put her pillow over her head, so she didn't see the Mirror Man convulse, or hear him grunt between his teeth as a cold glove closed around his heart. He did not cry out for help.

When the pain passed, he watched her as she slept.

Shadow Wrath

JOE DIDN'T LIKE FLYING. IT was unecological, uncomfortable and above all, it scared him. He didn't like the lurch as the wheels kissed the runway goodbye, the naked rivets on the fuselage or the way the wing flaps juddered as they retracted, and he didn't like the pressure of the seatbelt on his abdomen. He especially disliked the way the burps and farts of the other passengers were recycled through the air conditioning, enlivened by the occasional squirt of peppermint spray.

The lights were down low. Flat, micro-packaged dinners had been served to the passengers who had paid. Joe crumpled the empty packet of hypoallergenic airline snacks and put them in the plastic glass, which still held the dregs of pasteurised orange juice. He was in the centre seat, sandwiched between a chubby man staring through the window that looked over the starboard wing, and another fat flyer who had chosen the aisle chair. Gemma had been quiet at the airport and that troubled him.

'You hit me,' she said suddenly, as they passed over Germany. 'You almost killed me, except you knocked me free of my body and I hid.

'You know for a little bit, I thought I'd never existed until you. That all of the pictures and words I remembered had been dreams. What did I lose, Joe? What did you take away from me? Who are my family? What do I do? Where did I grow up? I had no past, so I didn't think I'd *been*, until I came to be right under your feet. You shouldn't have called me a bitch. That's what pulled it all together.'

'No,' croaked Joe.

'You want people to take you seriously?' said the shadow, relentlessly, from somewhere at the back of his head.

'Yes,' said Joe. The fat man at the window turned to look at him with a frown.

'You can't do that by hurting people,' said Gemma. 'That doesn't earn you respect. It just buys you hate.'

'I didn't have a choice,' said Joe.

'I did!' said Gemma, her voice like rough hair rubbing against velour. 'Until you took it away from me when you bashed my brains in.'

'I'm sorry!' squealed Joe. The man at the aisle cast a panicked glance in his direction. 'I am! I'm not joking. I'm not joking!'

But Gemma wasn't done.

The dark boiled beneath the chair. It oozed out of the armrest and ran like an oilslick up his sleeves. He tried to grab the seatbelt and pull the catch free, but it was fused to his shirt. Joe flung himself against the strap as the man by the window reached up and treble-clicked the orange call button. Joe's feet were glued to the carpet by the lightlessness beneath. He felt the shadows of his fingers clamp onto his fleshly hands like a clasping lover.

'Do you want to know what it's like?' said Gemma, from just above his shoulders. 'Do you want to know where I am not? I can show you. I can drag you out of this world.'

Joe felt the shadows rise.

The fat man at the aisle unhooked his stomach and stood up. He waddled away hurriedly in search of a stewardess. The man at the window sat helplessly beside the jack-knifing passenger. He tried to draw as far away as he could from the jerking, part-paralysed limbs. 'No!' screamed Joe. 'No, no, no!'

He felt the black draw over him, up his heaving chest, around his neck, over his lips and nose, asphyxiating him. But he still fought, and carried on fighting as it took his eyes and filled the little channels of his ears, spreading into his sinuses, leaving him mumbling and spasming as the passengers scrambled away and the cabin crew came running.

Intractables

BACK IN THE HOSTEL, ALL was quiet. She sat in the lounge in front of an old glass-screen television. 'Eithe,' said the Mirror Man. She ignored him. 'Eithe,' he said again.

'What?'

'Just talk to me,' he said.

'Why should I?'

'Please.'

She turned the television on so the images behind him would block him out. As she drifted off, a news reader explained how Suzana Grubjesic, the deputy prime minister, refused to publically acknowledge the independence of Kosovo. Serbia would not be invited into the EU, yet.

She had to turn it quite loud so she couldn't hear him.

Dead End

JOE CAME TO IN A warm, starched world. He felt
disorientated, dehydrated and dizzy. There was a faint
electrical hum, but it was a different frequency to the
aeroplane. He risked opening one eye. It was dim, but the
shadows were static and unthreatening.

'Gemma?' he said, but she did not reply. He lifted
his head.

The room was small, there were more than the usual
number of sockets in the wall and the bed had a metal
frame. From the low voices and the occasional bleep
outside, he guessed he was in a side ward of a hospital.
He reached over for the handset and pressed the call
button. As he waited for the nurse, he relaxed on to the

pillow. A feeling of relief filtered through his blood vessels, circulating and spreading from his calm heart to his tingling fingers and toes. He was in a hospital. He was still. He was safe.

'Mr King,' said the doctor, as he came through the door. Joe nodded weakly. The doctor, a tall, quietly spoken black man, reached for the light switch.

'No!' said Joe, but it was too late. He leaped to his feet, his head swimming, and he squinted in the glare. Gemma did not reach out of the sheer shadows and grab him. He blinked.

'I understand you had quite a flight,' said the doctor. 'Excuse me.'

He pulled a small torch from his pocket and applied his fingers to Joe's eyelids, inspecting the dilation of his pupils. Then he had the patient run through a series of counting exercises and simple questions, and finally he invited Joe to step across the room to display his balance and coordination. 'No harm done by the incident as far as I can see,' he said. 'And nothing in your history that suggests you are prone to seizures. Although I would recommend a scan, just to rule out any problems. And I will arrange a blood test, although you don't seem to have any viral symptoms. Do you remember what happened?'

'Yes,' said Joe.

'And how do you feel?'

'Not bad,' said Joe. He looked down at his feet, afraid of his own shadow, but it wasn't there. Relieved, he sat back down on the bed. She had gone. Maybe she hadn't ever been there.

The doctor looked at him curiously. 'Okay?' he said. Joe nodded. A sense of subtle wrongness was nagging at him.

The doctor put his pen away and dragged a plastic chair up to the side of the bed. He sat down. 'Most people,' he said, 'who had an attack and passed out on a plane would want to know the cause. You haven't asked what's amiss.'

'What's wrong with me?' said Joe.

'We don't know,' said the doctor. 'Physically, your blood pressure, your reactions, your vitals seem fine. You are exhausted, but that's it.'

'Good,' said Joe.

'Tell me,' said the doctor. 'Have you ever suffered from auditory or visual hallucinations?'

Joe froze as he realised what was wrong. His shadow wasn't there.

'Mr King?'

'Are you asking if I'm mad?' he said. His mind raced. No shadow. None at all. The light shone through him onto the tiles as if he wasn't even present.

The doctor laughed, gently, in a way calculated to put him at his ease. Joe bridled. 'Extreme fatigue can cause problems,' said the doctor. 'It can affect your memory and your senses.' He waited expectantly, but Joe, angry at the chuckle and afraid of the wandering shade, wasn't really listening.

Gemma could be anywhere, he realised, anywhere at all. What could stop a shadow?

'Mr King,' said the doctor. It was a prompt, not a question.

'Sorry?'

'I said, have you ever suffered hallucinations?'

Joe wondered whether it possible to hallucinate that something that should be there but wasn't. How would you explain that? 'No,' he said.

The doctor looked at him, level and unconvinced. Joe forced a shaky smile, and he relented. 'I'll book the tests,' he said. 'Tomorrow. Get some sleep.' He stood up. 'Goodnight, Mr King.'

'Please,' said Joe. 'Can you leave the lights on?'

The Return of the Prodigal Parents

IN THE MORNING, EITHE PICKED her new bag up and left the tower block. The train wasn't due to leave for hours, and she wanted to use up her remaining currency. She walked, for exercise and the chance to clear her head. Her route passed under a mass of scaffolding. When Eithe looked up, she saw a torn mess of rose-and-lemon brickwork. Struts of metal protruded and twisted out against the sky.

'A scar left by NATO,' said the Mirror Man.

'I know that,' she said. 'I'm not an idiot.'

She picked a café at random and looked at the menu. As she busied herself with arithmetic, she became aware that she was being watched. She lowered the menu, just a bit, to peep over the top.

There were two people sitting opposite her. They were more than middle-aged and quite elegant. The man wore a tailored shirt and the woman wore a demure black dress and glasses. Her hair was artistically curled. They prayed in quiet French. When they finished, the man caught Eithe's eye and smiled. She looked down at the menu again.

When the waitress came back, she ordered a glass of water and decided on a plate of bean soup and a salad, with extra bread to sop the juices. It would be nutritious and it would leave enough for a decent tip. A shadow fell across the table. She looked up into the amiable face of the Frenchman. He knotted his fingers bashfully.

'*Bonjour mademoiselle*. My wife and I—' he said. 'We want you to choose anything on the menu that you would like to eat. Anything at all. We will pay.'

'Oh,' said Eithe. She felt her eyes go round. 'That's very kind.'

'It is a Christian thing to do. You are alone and you are hungry.'

'Thank you,' said Eithe. 'I don't know what to say.'

'You do not need to thank us. I am sure it is part of the Lord's plan.'

Eithe, a born agnostic, felt awkward as well as grateful. The Frenchman went back to his table. Eithe knew that if she refused their offer, then they would be very offended. She ordered the soup and salad. When the meals ended, the couple joined Eithe at her table. The woman smiled at her in a vague, beneficent way. 'I am Jacqui and my husband is Philippe.'

'You travel?' said Philippe.

'Yes,' said Eithe.

'We are travelling as well. We have been to the great cathedrals of London and Berlin, Madrid and Rome, and now we come to see the works of the Orthodox worship.'

'Where are you from?'

'We live in Paris,' said the Frenchman.

As the talk continued and they asked each other polite questions, Eithe became aware of a gap in the conversation. They talked about their parents, now long dead, whose bequest had paid for their small pilgrimage, and about their cousins and nieces and nephews, but there was a space that the words would not fill. It reminded Eithe of how people avoided talking about her mother, who had once been but was there no longer. 'My mother was quite religious,' she said. 'But I'm afraid I'm not. I worry sometimes that she wouldn't be proud of me.'

'I am sure she would be,' said Jacqui.

'I suppose most parents love their children no matter what.'

Philippe grunted.

'Here's to our absent family,' Eithe said, and their faces tightened. 'You know, that reminds me. There's one story I never quite understood in the Bible.'

'What is that, *chère?*' asked Jacqui.

'The prodigal son.' said Eithe.

'Well you see,' said Philippe, 'it is about forgiveness.'

'"It was meet that we should make merry and be glad; for this thy brother was dead and is alive again; and was lost, and is found,"' quoted Jacqui. She looked a little bit pale.

'I don't know whether I'd be bitter if my son or daughter went off,' Eithe found herself saying. 'After all, your child is your child, whatever they have done.' The couple exchanged a glance. 'Do you have any children?' she asked, artlessly.

There was a pause.

'A son.'

'Any daughters?'

'No,' said Jacqui eventually. 'We had a daughter, but she was lost to us.'

'I'm sorry about that,' said Eithe. 'My mother died when I was born. I don't like saying I lost her. It sounds like I just left her somewhere without thinking. They say you don't miss what you never had. But I don't think that's true. I never knew my mother, but I miss her anyway. It must be so much worse to have known what it was like to have a daughter or a mother or father and then not to have them anymore.'

'Yes,' said Jacqui. She looked into her drink.

'If it hurts to love and lose, then I suppose the answer is to find it again. Thank you very much for the dinner,' she said, and she meant it. 'I've got to leave now, but I won't forget your kindness. You've been very generous. I'd be glad to have parents like you.'

Philippe said nothing.

'Look, I have to give you something to say thank you,' said Eithe. 'Just a little token.' She went into her bag and her fingers found a coil of warm metal. It felt right, so she pulled it out and put the ring on the table. The engraved cross winked in the light of the fountains.

Jacqui reached for it and held it up with a kind of wondering. 'Thank you,' she said.

'You're welcome,' said Eithe.

She put her coat on and set off for the station. She sat listlessly in the carriage, the Mirror Man watchful in the window. 'Eithe,' he said. 'You're changing things.'

'I don't want to talk to you,' she said.

'Okay,' he said. 'Then I'll wait until you're ready. I won't breathe a word at you. I have no power. Not even words. I'll leave you to make the verdict. You decide what happens to me. It's your choice.'

46

Awakenings

JOE WATCHED THE SINKING SUN from the ward window. He'd been moved in the morning, and now he was parked between two neighbours, one with a urine bag and another with a wheezing cough. They'd taken blood and monitored his heart, run him through a MRI scan and looked into every orifice, poked him, pricked him and even sent a psychiatrist to evaluate his mental state. He'd told them repeatedly that he felt fine, but they hadn't let him go.

And now the day was ending and the night was coming, and he didn't know what was worse – the light, which had made Gemma stronger or sharper, or the dark, which reminded him of the non-place she'd pulled him into.

He settled on to the bed and tried to relax. The patient next to him started snoring. The wall clock ticked. He hated it. The minute hand didn't work properly and it twitched backward before it told the second. Sometimes it didn't move at all for three seconds, and sometimes four, and dived forward through time with a shudder.

The light leeched away and his heart beat harder. It was a relief when he heard the soft sound of her footsteps sometime after midnight.

'I know you're awake,' said Gemma. She stood at the foot of his bed. Her outline was tenuous in the sombre ward, and if he narrowed his eyes she dissolved into the dimness, but she was there, an autonomous if insubstantial body.

'I knew you'd come,' he said. 'It was inevitable.'

'I want you to follow me,' she said.

'I don't want to.' When she reached for him, he jerked away involuntarily.

'You are going to,' she said. 'Not because it's written in the stars, but because you should.'

'No,' he said.

'Do it. Shadows get everywhere, even in locked rooms. You could be in the most secure bank vault in the world and I would still find you. Look in the dark places, where the bad things are, and I will be waiting for you. Come with me.'

'No!'

And then she started laughing at him. It was cruel and light, a happy torture which assaulted his ears. He pushed back the covers and slipped his trousers, shirt and shoes on, no pants, no socks. He moved as though he walking at an oblique angle to reality. There was no nurse at the desk as he left the ward and trailed Gemma's shade down the corridor. An orderly pushing a cage full of linen barely glanced at him as he passed.

'Funny,' said Gemma. 'A man following a shadow, when it should be the other way round.' She led him into another wing, down a deserted flight of stairs and through a set of double doors. She walked straight through them.

'I thought you were blind,' said Joe, as she guided him unswervingly.

'I found my body,' she said. 'I can feel where it is. I'm just going back to it.'

She passed through another door and Joe paused.

'I can't go through there,' he said. 'There's a keypad. They won't buzz me through.' But she pressed the green button on the other side of the doors and they parted for him. At each portal she opened the way, and he stalked past tired hospital staff, all busy with their own tasks, shuffling around in a weird medical dance. She brought him to the Intensive Care Unit, coaxed him around the vital wires and the loaded beds and then stopped.

Joe hated the hospital. He hated the bleeping monitors. He hated the ailing bodies. He especially hated the nearest patient, the only one with no teddies or cards, whose mouth was full of tubes, who breathed with mechanical bellows, and whose eyes would not close though the nurses tried to tape them shut. They stared vacantly at the sheen of a screen, and the staff had to dribble synthetic tears into them to stop them crusting over.

But Gemma was standing at the foot of a different bed. 'Here,' she said.

They both stared down at her supine body. Her eyes were still beneath their thin, translucent shutters. Her skin looked like thin smoke. She was not asleep and she was not awake. She was absent.

'This is what you did to me,' said Gemma-the-phantom. 'Do you see it now?'

Joe hunched over the bed. His back was bent and his hands splayed across the mass-laundered sheet as though it was a cloth upon an altar. There were little offerings all around her, mostly small toys, folded paper cranes, and a multitude of cards stuck to the board above her head, signed by friends and family.

'Gemma. It wasn't meant to be you. It was meant to be her. You were just in the way.' Joe lifted his head and his face was misery in flesh. 'It wasn't my fault. I am so weak.'

'Oh, but you did it anyway,' she said. She didn't sound angry, or bitter. She sounded flat with the magnitude of the accusation. 'No one else. You.'

He couldn't touch the shadow, so he reached for the hand of the unconscious woman and took it. 'It is my fault,' he said.

Her tendons and muscles felt flaccid and the small bones of her fingers were soft. He scrabbled but she flowed away, like water held too hard. And as her hand fell from his grasp, it tore something from him. Gemma made no reply. The shadow had gone.

Joe stood up. The movement atomised travel-dirt, the particles gathered in his hair, the grit of sleep, the insides of tired lungs, loose skin and sour sweat. The man with ragged hair and a seven-day beard gazed down at the sleeping woman. Her jaw was pinned and there were marks on the side of her head. With her eyes closed and her face still, Gemma was a living monument. Joe felt his chest ache. His ribs were a weak cage for his anger.

'It isn't fair,' he said, and for a moment, he managed to convince himself. 'It's because of everything.' Joe leaned in close. 'Don't you worry,' he whispered. 'I'm going to get her.'

'Hey.' Joe turned. The nurse stepped back. Joe looked horrific, like a thing gone feral. 'Hey, this is a secure unit!'

Then two things happened which distracted the nurses. The man in the next bed bucked and clenched, and then he lay deathly still as the monitor shrilled. A doctor ran in and tugged the curtain shut. More staff followed, one wheeling a defibrillator. Then Gemma made a noise. She was waking up.

In the confusion, Joe sprinted out of the ward, hammering on the door release buttons as he escaped. He barged out of a side door and found himself in the car park. The police might get there soon, but he took a moment to lift his feet one at a time and watch the way his shadow danced, his own again, subservient, safe.

There was only one place for him to go, and that was the flat. He knew that it wasn't wise; if Gemma remembered the attack and told the police, then it would be the first place they would raid. But he went there anyway, because it was what he had to do.

His key still worked. She hadn't changed the lock. A small, snowy tumble of envelopes greeted him as he pushed the door open. It was clear Eithe had not been back.

He gathered the letters into a sheaf and, as if he'd just come home from work, he went into the kitchen to make himself a cup of tea. He swept some of the rubbish from the table and put the letters down. Mould had colonised most of the crockery, but he drained the stagnant water from the sink and scrubbed a mug clean.

Most of the letters were bills and junk, which he discarded. Then he recognised the logo of a phone company and retrieved the envelope. It was not a network he used. Eithe was always careful to file away her bills and receipts, and insisted, despite the march of technology, on being posted a paper copy. He tore the most recent bill with fingernails bitten jagged.

The very first item read: 'Roaming Charge, EuroTel'. He quivered with rage as he eviscerated each envelope. The last entry was: 'Roaming Charge, Serbcom.'

A scream chased the acid up his throat.

For the Love of God

EITHE WALKED UNTIL HER SOLES blistered and then she limped. She sat down to take her shoes off and look at the damage, but she was afraid the wet feeling between her toes was blood, not sweat, so she got to her feet again and carried on. She was walking away from reflections. She knew the Mirror Man was dying and she didn't want to see it.

Macedonia was a patchwork of gold and green. She'd seen men walking with scythes over their shoulders. Small ponies grazed on the slopes, their skin twitching as insects landed on them. In the upper troposphere, wind tore the clouds to shreds, but the air around was still as Eithe crawled across the surface of the earth.

There was a huge cross on the peak of a hill. Maybe it lit up. Eithe didn't want to stay on the hillside at night to find out. She walked through a stony field full of dung and flies. They settled on her temples and around her neck where the sweat gathered and tried to suck the salt from her skin. She brushed them away but she didn't squash them. Her feet hurt like hell.

The sky was clear but the way was not. There was no path. Every so often, she found crucifixes painted in red on large boulders. There were tricky places where she had to navigate overhangs and little gullies that made her guess where the next mark would be. At one point, she had to climb a smooth, angled rock face by hanging onto a rope improvised from electrical wire.

She stopped at a spring to refresh herself, filled a bottle with water and poured it over her head. After a moment, she hobbled along a narrow woodland track and came out into the sunlight and thyme-scented air. The red-tiled roof of a monastery rose from a stumpy, straight-sided tower within a small clump of trees.

Eithe wasn't sure that she would be allowed into the building as a woman alone, but the day would soon die. She wondered if there were wild wolves in Macedonia. The front door was set in a whitewashed wall. Her knock was answered by a furious barking. She heard someone shush the dog and then the door grated over the cobbles as it swung open.

'*Dobro utro.*'

The words were sieved through a colossal beard which formed a semi-circle beneath a large nose. The voice was not unkind.

'I've come a long way.'

'So I can hear,' said the monk.

'Will you let me come in?'

He chuckled. 'Of course!'

He was shorter than Eithe and broad across the chest and swelling stomach. He wore a heavy black cassock and his hair, which was streaked grey like his beard, escaped from under his hat in a chaos of ringlets. His eyelashes framed his eyes like kohl. He didn't look anything like the ascetic, raggedy hermit she'd imagined. Although he was middle aged, plump and unfamiliar, Eithe was drawn to him. There was something beautiful about his crow's feet and the rich baritone of his laugh. His English was impeccable, his manner urbane.

'Come in,' he said, and he let her into the courtyard.

The ground was uneven and set with pebbles. The walls of the monastery were two floors high and a wooden gallery ran along the inside of the hexagonal space. The church was half as high again and plain from the outside. It was all built from hand-hewn wood and fixed with daub. In the middle of the yard, a huge St Bernard lolled in front of a dog house. He moulted and chewed on a ring of stale bread.

'What is your name?'

'I'm Eithe.'

'I am Valentin. Would you like to see inside the church, Eithe?'

'Yes please,' said Eithe, her tender soles forgotten.

They crossed the courtyard and entered the cool shadow. It smelled of old incense and there were urns of sand flanking the door. The sand was pocked with coins. 'We do not take payment,' said Valentin, as he picked up the stub of an almost extinguished candle. 'People who come here leave us tokens. That is all we live off, together with the kindness of the villagers.'

'We?'

'Bruno and I,' he said, as they passed under a stone arch and into the interior.

He showed her the paintings that danced across the walls, all the way up to the ceiling and across the slanting stonework. The colours were dulled by a patina of age, but Eithe could see the richness underneath, the clever way the artist shaded each fold of clothing, painted the large, guilty eyes of the penitents and pressed gold leaf to form haloes. The faces of the saints were earnest and anxious, while the angels wore compassionate, radiant expressions - even the smiting ones with swords and wings of fire. Eithe could have sworn that she saw the flicker of a feather in her peripheral vision, but it was only the whisk of the candle flame.

'In the Orthodox church, our paintings are not just supposed to be beautiful decoration,' said Valentin. 'Every one tells a story. When these were painted, not all could read. The peasants would listen to the stories from the Bible and then they could come here and see the icons, to remind them of what they had learned.

'Come and I will brew you some tea. It is a fine evening. We should sit outside.'

They sat at a picnic bench on the balcony and Eithe watched as he put three heaped spoonfuls of sugar in his cup. The tea had a wild perfume. 'It is thyme picked from these hills. Very good,' said Valentin. Eithe sipped it. When she looked at the dregs in her mug, she couldn't read them. The Mirror Man looked up at her blankly.

It was difficult to know what to say to the monk. When she thought about religion, Eithe had a confused notion of confession and priests, unleavened bread and guilt. But this man hadn't judged her at all. He just sat, smiled so that his eyes sparkled, and said, 'So tell me, what brings you so far?'

'I have a problem,' said Eithe, 'a few problems, really.'

'Don't we all?' said the monk, sympathetically. He steepled his fingers and set them under his chin in a listening pose.

'I'm trying to make a decision,' said Eithe. 'But I don't know how.' Down in the courtyard, Big Bruno shook himself. Eithe could hear his wet jowls slapping. The noise was incongruous in the quiet.

'Why not?'

'Because I don't trust myself.'

When Valentin chuckled, his entire body shook. He laughed from the soles of his feet to the top of his head.

'Ah, so you are a doubter. It is not orthodox to admit doubt,' said Valentin. 'But personally, I think doubt, like faith, is also something that takes strength. The easiest thing is not to think, but doubt and faith both thrive on contemplation. Once, I lived like everyone else. I drank alcohol, I worked hard, I had no one to tell me where to go or what to wear. I spent time with my family. I cooked, I walked, I went to the toilet, as we all do. But I was tired. It did not make me happy, or even content.

'So I decided to change. I worked hard to become a monk. I took my holy orders. I sacrificed the drink and money and the possibility of sex and the freedom to go where I wanted or wear what I wanted. But for me, that was no sacrifice at all, because I wanted to be wherever God, my Heavenly Father, sent me.

It is part of our tenet that we do not choose. We swear to abide by the rules of poverty, chastity and obedience. I am happy to wear the riassa every day, because now I don't have to stand in front of a mirror and put one tie after another to my shirt and worry about what is the best way to look.'

'But how did you know?'

'For some of us there is an epiphany. For me, not so much. I made a choice, which was to give up choice. It was a powerful decision, and day after day, second after second, I make it again and again. I reaffirm each hour, with my prayer, my thoughts, my breath. Long ago I took one turning on the path, which led to another and another, and always I stayed true. I could have gone another way, but I look back and I do not regret it.'

Eithe nodded. She understood.

'I think it's about time I went to sleep,' she said. 'I'm very tired.'

'Here is a key,' said Valentin. He pushed it across the table. 'If Big Bruno barks, he is chasing the birds. No one comes up here at night. There is nothing valuable that they can walk away with, apart from knowledge, and they need not steal that. You will be safe.'

The room reminded her of an old-fashioned orphanage. The bed was metal framed and squeaky. It was piled with hairy blankets. A crucifix was nailed to the wall and there was a bookcase. It was empty. There wasn't even a Bible. It smelled of spiders webs.

Eithe washed in cold water in a shower room and towelled herself down with one of the bedsheets. She left it to dry on the railing. Then she locked herself in the bedroom and buried herself beneath the hairy covers. But though there was no mirror and nothing to reflect once the light was off, she could not settle. She saw the Mirror Man every time she shut her eyes.

In the deepest part of the night, she left the room and walked down the stairs, her hand heavy on the rail.

Valentin was nowhere to be seen. She made her way into the church. She didn't light a candle stub, but she was careful to step around the excavated floor. She knelt because her heels hurt. The angels, saints and penitents were dark smudges across the walls.

'I don't believe in God,' she said. She stopped, feeling foolish, but then she forged on. 'I might as well sit by the spring and speak to the water, or sit in the wood and talk to a tree. But that's okay.

'For ages I thought if my mother hadn't had me, she would still be alive. Maybe I wouldn't be around, but instead, she might have given birth to all of the brothers and sisters I never had, and they would have given birth to all of the children that they will never have. Maybe an ending for one person is a beginning for many others. And I would never know to regret not living, because I wouldn't be alive to regret it. But maybes are for the future. Perhaps is not for the past. The past is done with. It can be reinterpreted, but it can't be changed.'

The Mirror Man looked out of the dusty metal candlestick, but he kept quiet, despite his distant degeneration. She was glad, because she wasn't speaking to him. 'I'm frightened. I've been frightened for a long time, of being alone, of not being alone.'

The angels and saints didn't look at her. Their eyes were fixed on each other, on Heaven and the swords.

'You can't choose to love. You can choose to acknowledge it or you can choose to ignore it until it dies of thirst and starvation. But you can no more refuse it than you can refuse to die and you can no more make yourself love someone than you force yourself to be born.

'I think I was on the verge of knowing it. Right on the edge, and then it was ruined. But now I have a choice. I have control, not just over myself, but over someone else. And if I keep it, he will die.'

She touched her forehead to the step. It was cool and crenulated against her brow. She didn't cry and she didn't laugh. The feeling was so huge that she couldn't move for a long time and she fell asleep on the hard floor.

Big Bruno woke her by barking like a coughing bull. She moved stiffly. Her muscles were still hard from the trek and her joints seized. She stopped by the urns and rolled a few colourful banknotes into a hollow cigarette and thrust it into the sand. The back of her feet rubbed against the inside of her shoes. It felt like her skin had sloughed off and the leather was scraping across her bare nerves.

Bruno was running in circles around his dog house. The chain was taut. It looked like someone lunging an ungainly pony. Valentin was filling his bowl, just out of range. 'Have you been praying?' he asked as he set the food down.

Eithe looked at the brown and white tail whirring through the air. The wag travelled from Bruno's hindquarters to the shoulders until the dog seemed to oscillate around his breakfast. 'In a way,' said Eithe.

'You have not found your answer,' said the monk.

'Not yet.'

'Ah,' said Valentin. 'Perhaps you should ask a friend.'

'I don't have any friends,' said Eithe.

'I'm sure you do.'

'No,' said Eithe. 'But thank you.'

She stumbled down the mountain with her head stuck in some dark dream.

It took hours to return to Prilep, and she was limping by the time she arrived. She travelled to Skopje on a rattling, old fashioned train with wooden seats and netted luggage racks, and then sat in the station staring at the times and destinations.

She stood there, tiny in a concrete building stained with decades of use, one undecided speck in a spill and spin of people who knew exactly where they wanted to go. She was afraid that, despite everything, the distance she'd travelled and the decisions she'd made, she hadn't really moved. She was in the same position she'd been in days ago, at Paddington Station – except that she'd moved a thousand miles sideways.

The phone trilled in her pocket. She pulled it out. 'Joe,' she said.

'I know you're not in England.'

'No,' she said. 'I'm not.'

'You tricked me. Why would you do that?'

'Really Joe?' she snapped. 'Really? Do you actually not understand?'

'You wouldn't come back,' he said, plaintively. 'Don't *you* understand? I'm coming—' he said, but she cut him off.

Eithe reined-in her sudden rage. 'Are you there?' she said to the Mirror Man. She was brusque and furious, but he felt a simple gladness that she was speaking to him.

'Yes.'

'We're going south,' she said. 'To Athens.'

Shadows Unshed

BEFORE HE'D LEFT, JOE HAD charted Eithe's progress on a map. It zigzagged down the continent, but it followed a roughly predictable path, and he followed it, taking a three-day, quick-changing journey overland.

Later and deeper and alone in former Yugoslavia, Joe was distressed by the profusion of jagged, violent sculptures, disturbed by the thickness of female ankles and the way everything bright and new seemed to be an anachronism, with tumbling Mars Bar wrappers and shiny Nike trainers creeping into a world time-locked in the seventies. He didn't like the heavy Cyrillic and the way the letters looked like chisel strokes in stone.

He was given a bunk with a curtain and drew it. His world was a tiny place, the length and breadth of a mattress. Louse called again. She'd called him every three hours to let him know there was no post for Eithe. 'I would look after you better' she said. There was a current of covetousness in her voice. Joe put the phone down without answering. He didn't want to speak to Louse, poor lost child.

In his flat, before he'd left, he'd asked her over to check on the post, to tell him where Eithe had called from. She had attempted to kiss him. He'd held her away from his face though she was a kitten trying to wash him with her tongue. He hadn't been disgusted or repulsed or even amused. He had felt sorry for her. Sorry that a girl could be silly enough to want to kiss him, and sorry that he was so contaminated with hate, with fear and with Eithe that he could not, would not, touch anyone else. Hate, he knew, was contagious.

He had put the girl away from him, but the hate had not gone away.

For years, he'd wanted to see this world. But it wasn't what he'd thought it would be. It was a mess of ugly concrete, of abandoned politics, of military jeeps, of cast metal statues of workers and soldiers covered in chewing gum, of buildings with war wounds and decaying monuments to dead leaders. But he recognised the ugliness as the indelible stain of history. He felt an affinity for the place. It, like him, was what it was. He wrote an email to Eithe.

Do you remember that night I asked you to give me your hand. I had a ring, the sort that came out of plastic eggs. I asked you to marry me, and I slipped it onto your finger. You just looked at the ring and said nothing.

Do you still have it?

Athens

THE CITY WAS A SWATHE of red roofs and white walls that spread out to the sea. 'Athens,' said the Mirror Man from the windows and the sunglasses of tourists. His voice was scratchy and faint. 'Eithe, we're in Athens. I remember it. We're in Athens.'

'It's okay,' said Eithe. 'I can hear you.'

'I know,' he said, weakly. 'I know.'

'I don't want to stay here long,' said Eithe. 'I've seen the pictures. The policeman on fire and protesters with blood on their faces.'

She roved through the simmering streets of Agios Nikolaos, Attica, and Syntagma. She searched through the streets where, only a few months before, the authorities had swept away the shards of Molotov cocktails.

'It's sadder than last time,' he said. 'More beggars. More dirt.'

'You can see the money has gone,' said Eithe.

'Go to the ruins,' he said.

Olive trees spread their silvered leaves over the streets. In the Metro, she saw reproductions of the Parthenon marbles and frescos showing women with bare breasts and bull dancers.

The caryatids troubled her. She wanted to lift up the stone and let them walk away. But she'd read the story of Atlas and now knew the dangers of lifting other people's burdens. The dust below the Acropolis was dry. Little dome-backed bugs scuttled out of the gaps between the stones and climbed up the spiny stems of grass.

'Nothing here,' he said. It was all he could manage.

She returned to the hotel.

'Miss Dord,' she heard, as she passed through the lobby. She turned her head toward the other woman sitting in a basket chair. It was Keane. She was not in uniform, but she rose crisply as Eithe recognised her. Her heels clacked on the tiles.

'Miss Dord,' she said.

'You,' said Eithe.

'I'm taking you in,' said Keane.

'That isn't the same as arresting me,' said Eithe. The questioning tone that Keane had thought so childish had vanished completely.

'I'm not afraid to make a scene,' said Keane. She unhooked a pair of handcuffs and reached for Eithe, who pulled away. Keane grasped her wrist hard and slapped the manacles on.

'Pull me through,' said Eithe quietly.

'Are you sure?' whispered the Mirror Man.

'Yes.'

So though it cost him dearly, the Mirror Man reached through the metal, whirled her over the edge of reality and then swung her back from the precipice. It was as fast as the passage from life to death. All Keane saw was Eithe shiver in the air and then the handcuffs jangled on the floor.

'You can try it again,' said Eithe. 'And it'll happen again, as many times as you want. I promise.' Keane sagged, and Eithe suddenly felt sorry for her. 'Let's sit down.' She led the policewoman to a glass table near the wall, and the older woman slumped down on to the basket chair cushion. 'Where's Erwin?' said Eithe.

'I had him transferred,' said Keane. 'I didn't want to. He was right to let you go.'

'What's going on, Detective Inspector?'

'Not a DI anymore,' said Keane. 'They were threatening my job. I quit.'

'They? Who are they?'

'Don't know who. Anonymous messages. First it was cash for information. I said no. They have money. Lots. They want to know what I know about him. Your fella. He has them scared. If he dies, no problem. If he wakes – trouble. I was to track anyone he liaised with. You. In case he spread information.'

'Have you told 'them' about me?' said Eithe.

'No. Was gonna bring you to them. A drop off point in London. Let them do their own damn dirty work.'

'Why?'

'They know where my kids are. School address, home address, afterschool tennis, football club, school bus, class timetable, doctor, everything.'

Eithe looked at the woman with her rugged features, her grey temples and double chin. Even with all her brawn, she looked defeated.

'I'm sorry about your children,' said Eithe. 'Really I am. But I can't let you take me in. I haven't got any information anyway.'

'Be useless soon anyway,' said Keane. 'He had a cardiac arrest.'

Eithe felt her own heart drain. 'When?' she managed.

'Three days back. Probably a gonner.'

'I have to go,' said Eithe. 'Now.' She pressed Keane's hand. 'Whoever 'they' are, you'll need someone who knows numbers. Go back to Britain, recruit Erwin and more like him. Watch your kids. If there's anyone who can keep them safe, it's you. And if I can help, I will. I promise. As long as you help me.'

Keane flinched.

'No,' said Eithe, gently. 'I'm not bribing or bargaining with you. I'm telling you because I should have told someone weeks ago, but I didn't, and I'm afraid he attacked Gemma Imai because I wouldn't speak up. There's a man called Joe King. He was my fiancé. I want him arrested. He's threatened me and hurt me, and at one point he had a firearm. Remember his name.'

Keane nodded miserably.

'Goodbye,' said Eithe. She did not look over her shoulder as she entered the lift. As she packed, Eithe decided where she was going. When she came down from the room, Keane had gone.

The Isle of Venus

EITHE'S LAST VIEW OF ATHENS was of the churning water pushing the docks into the distance. As the bow wave rippled off into the Mediterranean, she opened her mouth to taste the breeze.

The Mirror Man spoke from the rail. 'I can't do it again,' he said. 'Can't – take you through.'

'I know,' said Eithe. 'When you saved me from the bullet – after that you had the heart attack. It hurt you. But you did it again to free me.'

'You knew the way.' There was a torturous pause before he said, 'But you tore it up.'

Eithe smiled sadly. 'I memorised the journal,' she said. 'It was the only part of you I had.' She counted the entries

off on her fingers. 'The card for the Rainbow, the picture
of the fresco in Würzburg, the ticket for the spa in Bad
Gastein, the Venetian bead, the postcard from Rijeka, the
pine needles from Sophia. You took piece of brick from
the NATO bombsite in Belgrade and in Prilep it was a
wooden pendant with an orthodox saint. When you were
here you tried to sketch the Venus de Milo. Don't give up
the day job.'

He laughed painfully. 'Where now?'

'Milos,' she said.

'Last stop,' he said, and then he lapsed into silence.
Eithe sailed the blue sea beneath a cloudless sky.

The ferry docked at a port town where she found an
apartment with blue shutters. It took a long time. The
villas were all shut for the season and many of the owners
had migrated elsewhere, or were busy doing the jobs
that kept them solvent when the mass of tourists were
shivering at home. But the little old lady Eithe found was
incredibly happy to hand her the key. There wasn't much
money to be made sweeping empty buildings.

It was a simple space with white walls and a tile floor.
The chairs and tables were wicker and the shelves held
seaside trinkets like shells, pebbles, dried sea horses and
sea stars. Among them was a tiny replica of the statue
of Venus.

'Aphrodite,' Eithe said. 'She's the goddess of love, but
she hasn't got arms. She can't embrace.'

'It's where it ended,' he said, faint and unfocused. 'Just
before it ended. There was the Venus. Not the real one.
Little ones. Everywhere. The same size as the dinosaurs.'

'Shush,' she said, but there was no anger left in her. 'We
will find who you are. I know it.'

'I remember this island,' he said, groggy. 'It's warm here.' She was distracted and didn't reply. 'What are you thinking?' he said.

'I'm going to have to face him,' said Eithe.

'Joe? No,' said the Mirror Man. 'He's insane.'

'But in a way I understand,' said Eithe.

'Please don't,' said the Mirror Man.

'Why?' said Eithe. 'Because you're afraid he'll kill me and you won't know what will happen to you then?'

'No,' said the Mirror Man. Then he saw her face. 'Yes,' he said, honestly. 'Yes, I'm afraid of that. But I also don't want to see you hurt. Eithe, I—'

'What?'

'You're better than you think. You're better than him.'

'I know.'

'I pushed your reflection aside. When I met you. I worried I'd thrown some part of you away. Couldn't have been more wrong. I just packed you in tight. Now you're expanding. Now you're becoming.'

'Shhh.'

She took out her phone and sent a message. It was two lines long.

I am on Milos. Come and find me.

She thought about Joe and a quiver of something inexplicable ran through her. It took her a while to realise that it wasn't fear. It was anticipation.

She checked her emails but there was only one message.

Dear Eithe,

The most wonderful thing has happened!
My Maman and Papa have written to me. I am not sure if
I am yet forgiven, but they say there is money I am to inherit.
Perhaps it will be enough to save the Rainbow. If your most
kind offer to us is still available, we would like you to perhaps
work on our accounts. We will pay. It is good to have an
outside eye.

Juliette.

'You see?' said the Mirror Man. 'You changed things.'

Then she slept without nightmares.

In the morning, she hired a moped and drove to where the statue of Venus was discovered by a peasant almost two-hundred years ago. The speed limit was set at forty kilometres an hour, but the locals belted along at eighty. She had to use a mantra to make sure she stayed in the right lane and didn't crash: right is right, right is right, right is right.

There wasn't much in the ruins. The site was a dusty bowl. Torpid green and brown lizards, fresh from hibernation, licked their lips as they sat on the stones and watched her. She picked over the ground, eyes wide for any clues, but there was nothing. Just dirt. Her haunches hit the dust and she had to dash away tears of frustration and wasted effort. After a moment, she pulled out her phone.

'Well this is it,' she said. 'Now you've seen the place, do you remember?' The Mirror Man managed a shallow shake of his head. 'I need more,' she said. 'You need to give me more. Is there anywhere else?'

But his eyes were closed and he did not reply. Eithe felt numb. It was too late. 'I hoped once I got here it would all sort itself out,' she said.

'Well it kind of did,' whispered the Mirror Man.

'So it's ended then,' she said. 'We've run out of options. We aren't at a crossroads. We've reached a dead end.'

'You don't sound happy. I thought you'd be happy. This way, you don't have to make a decision.'

'I wanted to choose,' she said. 'For the first time ever, I wanted to choose, and the choice has been taken away.'

'I understand,' said the Mirror Man, and for once he didn't sound sarcastic.

'How do you feel?'

'Cold,' he said.

'I let you down,' said Eithe.

'No,' said the Mirror Man. 'You tried. You did exactly what I wanted. And that didn't work.' Then he jerked and gasped, as though he was coughing inwardly, and then there was a gurgle. Eithe felt horribly impotent as she watched him drown in his own fluids. His throat undulated and bulged, his head pulled up. Then, with a convulsion, he was back. 'I'm okay,' he said, in a crackling voice.

Eithe pulled away. 'This is going to keep happening,' she said, 'isn't it?'

'Yes,' he said, 'until it stops. I'm sorry…'

'Part of your consciousness is in me,' she said. 'And I'm rejecting you. I can't stop it.'

He managed a nod.

She put the phone away and sat, hunched in the dirt. After a while, she dusted off her hands and found her feet.

She returned to the village where old men played backgammon under awnings and stray cats gathered in the square for a daily meal of dried biscuits and a bucket of water. Goats grazed in the field beneath her balcony. The sea was a deep glorious sapphire. She sat alone as night fell and plumes of yellow smoke flared from the sulphur mines in the distance.

She thought about Juliette, her parents and the monk Valentin who was content to dress in a riassa – brief relationships, all of them. She felt a bit sad, because she knew she probably wouldn't see them again. When she went inside, she was reluctant to look at the television in case she saw something dead looking back, in case she saw the corpse that would decay and reveal the smiling skull. But the Mirror Man was still alive, just.

'I want you to leave,' he said. 'I don't want you to face him. Just go.'

'No,' said Eithe. 'I want to help you.'

'You won't be able to if you're dead,' he said.

Eithe did not want to argue. 'This is a nice place,' she said. The Mirror Man was as insubstantial as a hologram. She only saw him because she expected to see him. His face seized for a moment. 'It hurts,' she said.

'Yes.'

'I'm sorry.'

'It's okay.'

She studied him, the deep crevices around his mouth, the way the skin hung loose from his jowls, the way the fat had burned away like wax, leaving hard bone.

'Do you want to know why I followed you?' he said. 'You and nobody else? It wasn't just because you were open to me. It's because most of the time, when you look into someone's eyes, you see yourself reflected right back, and because most of the time, when you're speaking, they're waiting for their turn. But you really saw me, even when most of me wasn't there. I don't know why you think you can't love, or why you think you don't deserve it.'

Her feet made faint sounds on the tiles. She went over to the television and lifted her hand to the surface. Static spat when she touched his face. 'I haven't found the way to restore you.'

'That was because there isn't a way, Eithe. I'm afraid that was my biggest lie, more than the fraud and the emails, and anything else.

'Eithe, when I die, I want you to take my money,' he said. 'All of it. I want you to go as far as you can and stay away from him. I want you to do it as soon as possible before they freeze my account.'

'But it's yours,' she said, disturbed.

'No it isn't. And even if it was, it doesn't mean anything, after a while,' he said. 'When you have more than enough, the rest is just numbers. And I want you to find out how much I helped steal. Give it back.'

'I'm not going to run anymore,' she said. 'And neither are you. I'm going to stay here and think about how to help you for as long as I can. I will find a way. And if he catches up with me, I'll deal with it.'

'When he comes for you, touch a mirror,' said the Mirror Man. 'And if he does something, I'll move you.'

'Don't you dare,' said Eithe. 'Don't you bloody dare. I'll kill you if you do.' He laughed at that. 'I'm serious,' she said.

'Eithe,' he said, and then he stopped as though he was on the cusp of saying something too big for words.

'Yes?'

'Goodnight.'

The Chosen Path

THE PLANE TOUCHED DOWN AT the island's tiny airport. Joe disembarked and hired a car to take him from place to place. He bought a knife in a little supermarket. It was made for paring fruit, but he knew that if he stabbed hard enough it would penetrate Eithe and she would bleed. To kill her he would have to cut her many times. He would have to puncture her guts and pierce her crotch and maybe, at the end, push it into her throat. He considered the act in a vague, flavourless way. Now he was here, he did not want to hurt other people, not any more.

But he had no choice. He had made his plan and it had to happen. How could other people take him seriously if he couldn't even trust himself to fulfil his mission?

Joe found Eithe's apartment by asking around. In a small village, the locals knew her by face if not by name, and they were curious about the tall, quiet, lone woman. He held back tears as he told her hosts he was her boyfriend, here to surprise her with a gift. They spoke poor English, but they drew a rough map on the back of an envelope and he climbed back into the taxi. She had gone to Sarakiniko, a geological peculiarity, a bright white beach on the north side of the island.

The sun was draining to a dark orange by the time he found her. Sarakiniko was a blasted, beautiful moonscape. Little grains whispered against their big brothers, wearing them down into more sand. The shape of the breeze was carved into the stone. Joe walked among the air-smoothed boulders and gulleys with a wrinkled nose. Someone had pissed up a rock wall in one of the little caves. Something lay rotting on the shore.

Eithe was up to her chest in water and her hair was tied tightly at the back of her head. All around her, ripples moved out. She was framed by the weird, wind-carved curves in the rock. She was wading through the water as though she was trying to find something with her feet. Her back was to him.

He had his knife in his hand. His palms were wet against the plastic handle. If he pushed through the water fast enough he could catch her before she swam away. Then he could ram the blade between her ribs. Maybe she would struggle, but he could hold her down until she choked. He imagined her hair swirling in the sea. The thought that has sustained him over several thousand miles was stale. It didn't excite him anymore. Here and now he felt tired. He wanted to wail, to warn her so she could run, but his tongue was dying because nothing he could say could change the future. He wanted her back, as she used to be.

He took a deep breath and paused at the point where the surf sucked at the sand. Eithe did not turn. 'Hello Joe,' she said.

'Hello Eithe.' He tensed, ready to leap and pin her down, but she did not run.

'Do you have the gun?' she said.

'No,' he said. 'I broke it and buried it before I went back to England. They would have arrested me at customs.'

'But you have something else,' she said.

'I have a knife.'

'You won't hurt me,' she said, and she turned around.

As she came ashore, the sanguine sea moved her from side to side so she seemed to dance slowly as she went. Behind her, the water burst into flame as the sun hit the horizon. Joe recoiled and narrowed his eyes until all he could see was a dark shape wavering in front of the blaze, like a spot on the surface of the sun.

When he opened them again, he saw her standing on the uncertain ground, sometimes ocean, sometimes land. She smiled at him. She looked so sure.

She said, 'You know, I've been thinking. When you met me, you said it was too much of a coincidence that I came to the same city you did. Valentin the monk would say that it's God's Plan, and I think that Juliette, with her romance, would say it was destiny. I don't believe in either of those things.

'But I do believe in probability. Coincidence is just a case of numbers. There are a finite number of places in the world and a finite number of people to encounter within them. It would be far more remarkable if there were no coincidences at all.

'There's a one in twenty-six chance that you will share the first letter of your name with your lover. There's a one in seven chance that you were born on the same day of the week. There's a one in three-hundred-and-sixty-five chance that you share a birthday. That doesn't mean that you are destined to be together. When I was conceived, one out of a hundred-million sperm made it to the egg. There were many million other versions of me who never existed. Compared to the odds of that, meeting you wasn't such a huge coincidence. So I stopped thinking about how amazing it was that I'd met you. I met you, and that's all that matters.

'And that's why I came here, in a roundabout way. It's a coincidence, and that isn't so strange if you think about it.'

'Eithe,' he said, as though he could turn her back into the weak, meek girl he'd known by invoking her name.

'Joe, I don't love you anymore. I haven't even liked you for a long time. But I think we were drawn to each other because we were both so alone.

'You were good in some ways. I've learned a lot from you, about how to live lightly and not to hurt the world. You can go back to that, if you really want to. But all we really had in common were our nightmares. And mine don't scare me anymore.'

'This has to happen,' said Joe.

'There are some things that have to happen, and some things we can change. You know this is the second one, not the first. And that is why you won't hurt me.'

Joe looked at her. The girl who'd believed in him was gone. The girl who had been afraid of him was gone. If he killed her, he would be killing a stranger. He knew he had lost her forever.

'You can choose,' said Eithe. 'You can.'

Joe felt the world expand. It poured out in every direction, terrifying and brilliant. He felt as though he had crawled out of a cave or broken the surface of a cold pool and reached the air. The knife hit the sand.

'I'm sorry,' he said, as he hollowed out.

'Go home, Joe,' she said, and it was final.

He turned around. He would go back to Britain and back to the flat where he would wait for the police to arrive. Then he would give himself up, not because it must happen but because he was tired and too heavy with guilt to run.

He left the blade to corrode in the salt air and trudged away.

52

Solutions

EITHE WATCHED JOE WALK AWAY, and he took the last trailing rags of fear with him. In its absence, she felt a wash of strange sadness, bittersweet, as though a good film had ended at an unexpected point.

'It wasn't the victory— you wanted,' said the Mirror Man. His voice was the sound of sliding particles, barely audible.

'It was, but it's not important anymore,' said Eithe.

She sat down with her feet just beyond reach of the small surges of salt water.

Gulls perched and bickered on the cliffs. The water looked like wrinkled pink silk. Sand clotted the backs of her legs like crusty stockings. The grains prickled as they rubbed against the little hairs, but she didn't want to separate herself from the water. She didn't want to pull away from the Mirror Man. She let the brine inch up to her feet. In the distance, a traditional *kaiki* fishing boat cut the sea like a set of shears. In the shallows, sea urchins rippled with organic fluidity.

Her gut did a fandango.

'You're my best friend,' she said. 'I hated you for a bit, but you are.' She let out a sob.

'Don't be sad,' he said, teasing. 'I'm dying, not you.'

The tide towed a little further up the beach. It folded around her like soft armour. 'Do you think you're gone?' she said.

'Not yet,' he said, 'but not far off. Maybe an hour. Maybe less.'

'I'll stay with you,' she said.

'Don't,' he said. 'You don't have to. I don't want you to see it.'

'No,' she said.

'So you've grown yourself a backbone,' said the Mirror Man. It took longer for him to speak. There was a gap between every word.

The water covered her ankles. She regarded his profile, with its sunken cheeks and translucency.

'I've been here before,' said the Mirror Man, and the memories came back, spilling inside him like sand spread by wind. 'Back when I was young, when I liked music and rollercoasters and football cards and dinosaurs. Oh, I really liked dinosaurs. I buried one in the sand here and I never found it again. I left a little bit of me here. I came back to find it on my own, when I was older, with just a backpack. The journey ended here.

'After that, I had to grow up. I had to get a job. I was good at my job, and I gave my life to it. I worked, I got up, I went home, I slept, I worked, I got up, I went home, I slept, I got up and I made money. I got good. And then they noticed me and started asking me to do things, and I said *yeah, sure*, because I was a realist, and you don't get on in life without making some moral compromises. And if the things they asked me to do didn't seem quite right, I didn't ask any questions and told myself that it was fine, I was a businessman, and it was how things were done.

'And then one day I woke up and I realised I didn't really like myself very much. In fact, I loathed myself. I wanted to go back to before.'

'Why?'

'I went to work, because that was all I could do. And then, when I was looking through the papers, I found my employers had tracked down my tax haven accounts and the names I used for them. I suppose the vice was closing in around them. With all the austerity and cuts the public were less and less inclined to let fraudsters get away with it and things were getting sticky. So they tied my fake names to all of their fake accounts, the ones they used to syphon funds away from our clients. And I knew I was fucked.

'I remember leaving the office. I remember feeling sick and breathing too fast. I leaned against a window and it felt as though there was a hurricane behind me, a screaming gale of loneliness and anger. It picked me up and carried me through the glass. I wanted to go. I wanted to flee. I wanted to get away from the blank faces and the blank spreadsheets and the commute. But mostly I wanted to leave myself.

'Then I found you. Now I don't want to leave here. I like it here. I like being with you. I don't want to go back.'

They sat, silent and staring, she at him and he at her, as the water licked at her bellybutton and stroked her floating ribs. The sea had risen to her hips. Little fish sucked at her toes. Time stretched and folded until it was as thick as toffee.

'You didn't want me to find your name,' said Eithe. 'You were running, just like me.'

'Yes,' said the Mirror Man. 'I thought if I went far enough I wouldn't be able to feel it. I thought if I pushed you on and on we'd reach the point where the bonds between my body and whatever part of me is here would snap. That's why I did the worst thing. That's why I didn't tell you about Joe. I was afraid you would stop. I knew that while he was chasing you, you'd carry on.

'But everywhere is too close. I could buy a spacecraft and blast off and fly a million miles, and I'd still know the moment when my body failed. I can feel it somewhere remote. My blood is slowing down. My body is somewhere, with its liver and kidneys working on nothing, recycling the same liquid around the bloodstream over and over until it becomes poison. It's a husk. I don't want it anymore. Now I just want to leave it behind.'

'I'm sorry I didn't help you.'

'You did.' He smiled, feeble but heartfelt. 'You did. I'm not – I'm not angry now. It wasn't the place I needed to find. It was the person to be with. I suppose some people… travel to find themselves. But I – didn't need that. I needed you.'

The little hairs on her spine lifted. Deep in the pool of her memories, something surfaced like a dark dorsal fin. 'You took me through the surface,' she said, 'when I needed to escape. You brought me through to the other side. I could pull you back to this side.'

'I know you want to … help, but … I don't think that's possible, Eithe,' he said tenderly.

But Eithe was tired of worrying about impossibility. She was tired of being told to do, not to do, what to do.

'I can,' she said, utterly sure. She reached into the water, closed her fingers around his hand and hauled him out of the sea.

The Mirror Man moved up with the wave, but stayed, glittering, as it ebbed back, so two torsos, one dark and one luminous, emerged from the surface. Shorn of the angularity, the tautness and the fierceness of his driven soul, he was almost beautiful. She held his watery hand gently.

'You did it,' he said, amazed.

'You taught me the trick of it,' she said.

'It is almost too late,' he said, through liquid lips. 'But I don't mind. I remember my name now.'

He leaned in gently to whisper it.

'Wait,' said Eithe. She placed her free hand on his cheek. 'I haven't saved you yet. You don't need to be here. You need to be in your own body, and I can give you the push you need.'

'I don't want to go back. I don't want to leave you by yourself.'

'I don't want you to die,' said Eithe. 'And I have to learn to be with myself.'

'You would let me go?' he said. 'And be alone again, after everything?'

'Yes,' she said.

She looked into his eyes, and for the first time, they did not show fear or self-involvement or frustration. They held something she had never seen before, but she recognised it all the same. She knew a moment of total anguish, and she wanted to say, 'Then don't,' but she knew if she had, he would have stayed. She could have held him until he died, then she would have had him always and lost him forever.

'What if I get lost?' he said.

'Follow the trail we made. Everywhere we've been has showed us the way back. And when you wake, call Erwin, like we promised. And you'll tell them everything. If you go now, I'll come and find you. Then I will learn your name.'

'You promise?' he said.

'Yes,' she said. 'I will. When I have finished my journey.'

'Okay,' he said.

'Okay,' she said. 'Ready?'

He nodded, and together they rose.

They stood, streaming in the twilight, the stars shining through him. For a moment each behaved as though they had never seen the other before, a fleeting meeting of the eyes, a turn away like strangers in the street. But their hands were pressed together, water against flesh.

He asked, 'There was something you never told me. 'Who were you thinking about that night in Rijeka? Will you tell me?'

She was lost for a moment, and then a smile filtered through her features until her eyes were polished copper. 'Perhaps I will, maybe I won't,' she said as though each word was delicious to her.

'Please.'

For just a few moments, she drew him close and felt his thin meniscus press against her body. And then she flung him away so that his self and the saltwater crashed back into the sea and then he was gone, outside and in.

'It was someone I haven't met yet,' she said to the foam. When it cleared, leaving a thin slick across the sand, she saw her own curious eyes, her dripping hair flaring down her back like the hood of a cobra. 'I'll see you soon, Mirror Man,' she said.

A pressure she hadn't even been aware of eased. She felt her self unfurl. She looked out to the horizon, and then further still, to the deep sky. She was alone but she was not lonely, not any more.

SOLUTIONS

Now

EITHE SAT AT THE BREAKFAST table in the new
flat. It was airier then her old one and there were no cracks
in the walls. It was furnished the way she wanted it, with
ornaments here and there – most of them from parts of
Europe. One was a mask of a crying clown. There was a
newspaper open in front of her. It was only a small article,
because it was only big news for a small group of people.
There was no picture. It simply told of how Joe King, 29,
of so-and-so street, Manchester, had pleaded guilty to a
count of grievous bodily harm and several other offences
relating to attacks on two women, and that he was serving
a seven year sentence at a medium security prison.

She took out a pair of scissors and carefully cut the
article out. She glued it in a scrap book. This one was new.

The phone went and she picked it up without
any hesitation.

'You ready, chick?'

'Yep.'

'I'm in the car park. Taxi's waiting'

'I'll be there in a minute.'

Gem was waiting in the back seat. She looked different
from how she had been, before the night out, before Eithe
had gone abroad and blown like a leaf across the continent.
There was something subtly wrong about her skull and
she spoke slowly, as though she had to chew over every
thought, and her words sounded blunted when they came
out. But she was alive.

'Royal Courts of Justice,' said Eithe, and the
driver nodded.

The car coasted along.

'Thank you for coming with me,' said Eithe to Gemma.

'Hey, I invited myself. I know you don't need me to
hold your hand,' said Gem. 'I am as curious as you.'

'I'm not sure about that,' laughed Eithe.

'I'm going to avoid courts from now on,' said Gemma. 'Twice in one year is too much.'

'Yes, but we're just spectating this time.'

'Are you all packed for Paris?'

'Not yet. I wanted to do this first, before I left. It's a bit full at the moment. Juliette said getting a room wouldn't be a problem, but when I checked online every bed was booked up. It's been busy since the renovation. I'm looking forward to seeing her, though. I told her I'd cook this time.'

'I'm sure she'll squeeze you in somewhere,' said Gemma. 'I think you're going to be mothered within an inch of your life.'

Eithe made a rueful face, but in truth, the idea appealed. She'd never been mothered before, not really. It would be interesting to see what it was like.

'Oh, look!' said Gemma.

The Royal Courts of Justice were immense and beautiful, but after all the tiled floors and high, vaulted ceilings she'd seen, Eithe wasn't intimidated any longer. It was strikingly different from the Crown Court she'd attended for Joe's sentencing – that had been a brick-built box, while this looked like a white palace from the outside, with spires and arched windows and doors, and the courtroom, one of many, resembled a library. Even the court room itself was different, in function as well as form. There was no jury, but there were two judges in the room. This was the last court before the House of Lords, and the second highest in the land. Recently, the government had allowed filming at the Court of Appeal, and Eithe half-hoped and half-feared that the cameras would be there, because she knew this was important, and that people needed to know what happened, quietly and covertly, to their money and their livelihoods, but she felt a flutter of her old shyness at the thought of being caught on film.

She'd worried for a while that they would call her as a witness, but neither Erwin or Keane had linked a Miss Dord with the fraud case, except as a dead-end lead generated by confusing CCTV footage.

Keane wasn't in the court room. She would testify at a different date, on different charges. Erwin was present though, and he'd got rid of the comb-over in favour of a close trim. He met Eithe's eye as she took her seat in the public gallery, but he did not acknowledge her in any other way. She was equally as controlled, and she moved her eyes to where the appellants were sitting.

There were several – she recognised the CEO from the newspapers, and other high-ups in the banking sector. They all wore very nice suits but they did not look smug now they were firing their last salvo against an army of accusations of fraud, misconduct and breach of trust. The whole affair was complex and although Eithe could follow the numbers, she got lost in the legalese. She watched with a stony face, and, after the hearing had been running few hours, she felt Gemma sag against her.

Then he walked in, and suddenly she was wide-awake and leaning forward. Beside her, Gemma started.

'Is that him?' she whispered.

Eithe nodded.

He was there, he was real and he was solid.

They read out his name – Richard Edwards. She smiled at the mundanity of it after all the mystery.

She didn't catch everything during the cross-questioning, because he spoke quite quietly. He looked tired but determined.

It had been more than a year since she'd pushed him through the barrier between here and out-there, digging him out of her core and flinging him back into his own body. She didn't know what had happened after that, whether he'd smashed into himself and woken with a gasp, his organs shocked into operation, or if he'd slowly taken command of his flesh again, unfurling slowly inside his bones, nerves and muscles. She hadn't known, until the case started, if he'd upheld his side of the bargain, but here he was, testifying.

She'd forgotten how tall he was.

Strange, she thought, that for a lot of the time they'd been together, she'd hated seeing his face, but now she couldn't look away. She studied the lines of his nose, the way his cheekbones jutted and the dark circles around his eyes.

'When will we know?' Gemma hissed, 'whether they've got them or not?'

Eithe shrugged.

'This is the last hurdle,' she said. 'We've got this far.'

The hearing was not over when the Mirror Man stepped away from the wooden box, but Eithe touched Gem lightly on the shoulder and whispered, 'I'm going to find him.' Gem nodded, and Eithe shuffled her way out of the public seats.

Back in the corridors, she paused and cast around. She had no idea where he would be. A wave of panic engulfed her – what if she didn't catch him? What if she never saw him again? She stood in the corridor, listening to the echoes of footsteps, and closed her eyes.

Then she remembered the cigarettes, and she started running.

She found him in the designated smoking area, sparking up. There was a police officer next to him. His hands were shaking as he cupped them, trying to protect the match from the breeze.

'You're Rich,' she said.

'Not anymore,' he said, not looking up.

For a long, horrible moment, she thought he didn't know her, that everything they'd been through was a mad phantasmagoria. Then he lifted his head.

'Eithe,' he said.

'Hi,' she said.

They stared at each other levelly for too long. His face was unreadable. A hundred and twelve questions crowded up Eithe's throat, but only one managed to squeeze through.

'Do you think they'll go to jail?' said Eithe. He nodded.

'I'll see them there,' he said, and her heart shrivelled. 'It was the only way. They thought they were immune because if they fell, they'd take me with them. It didn't occur to them that it also worked the same in reverse. Ow, god!'

He dropped the stub of the cigarette and sucked on his singed fingers.

'You'd better pick that up,' said Eithe. 'Or they'll do you for littering.'

He laughed.

There was another, second-stretching silence.

'I'm going to be inside for some time,' he said. 'I've been sort of looking forward to today. It's been a bit of a break. I have to go back now.'

'Yes,' said Eithe. 'I know.'

'I'm sorry,' he said. 'You've done so much for me and I haven't been much of a friend to you.'

'You've gone from never saying sorry to saying it far too often,' said Eithe.

'I missed you,' said the Mirror Man – she still couldn't quite think of him as Richard. 'Why did it take you so long to find me?'

'I had my own things to sort out. I've been learning to be by myself.'

'And how is it?'

'Not bad. I quite like me, after all.'

'So you should.'

He was a metre from her, but it could have been a hundred and fifty kilometres for all that she could cross the distance. And he did not seem inclined to reach for her. Instead, he stood, contrition writ in the lines on his face, and he couldn't help but look down.

'This could be where it all ends,' he said, unable to meet her gaze. It was not disinterest that kept his eyes glued to the floor. It was deep shame. Eithe saw it and she understood.

'No,' she said.

She reached up and took his head in her hands. They were almost of a height, and he was whole and healthy. It suddenly felt entirely natural and right to touch him. His cheeks were clean-shaven and his skin felt warm and it flushed beneath her fingers as though he had a fever. Gently, she eased his face toward her, cupping her fingers to funnel his gaze. He didn't resist as his pupils latched on to hers.

'No,' she said again. 'This could be where it all begins.'

NOW

Printed in Great Britain
by Amazon.co.uk, Ltd.,
Marston Gate.